Beauty and the Beast
(Faerie Tale Collection)

"Jenni James takes this well loved faerie tale and gives it a paranormal twist. Very well written and hard to put down, even on my cruise vacation where I had plenty to do. Looking forward to others in Jenni's Faerie Tale series. A great escape!"

—*Amazon reviewer, 5-star review*

**Pride & Popularity
(The Jane Austen Diaries)**

"This book was unputdownable. I highly recommend it to any fan of Jane Austen, young or old. Impatiently awaiting the rest of the series."

—*Jenny Ellis, Librarian and Jane Austen Society of North America*

"Having read several other Young Adult retellings of Pride and Prejudice - I must admit that Pride and Popularity by Jenni James is my top choice and receives my highest recommendation! In my opinion, it is the most plausible, accessible, and well-crafted YA version of Pride and Prejudice I have read! I can hardly wait to read the [next] installment in this series!"

—*Meredith, Austenesque Reviews*

"I started reading Pride and Popularity and couldn't put it down! I stayed up until 1:30 in the morning to finish. I've never been happier to lose sleep. I was still happy this morning. You can't help but be happy when reading this feel good book. Thank you Jenni for the fun night!"

—*Clean Teen Fiction*

Northanger Alibi
(The Jane Austen Diaries)

"Twilight obsessed teens (and their moms) will relate to Claire's longing for the fantastical but will be surprised when they find the hero is even better than a vampire or werewolf. Hilarious, fun and romantic!"

—*TwilightMOMS.com*

"Stephenie Meyer meets Jane Austen in this humorous, romantic tale of a girl on a mission to find her very own Edward Cullen. I didn't want it to end!"

—*Mandy Hubbard, author*
of Prada & Prejudice

"We often speak of Jane Austen's satiric wit, her social commentary, her invention of the domestic novel. But Jenni James, in this delicious retelling of Northanger Abbey, casts new light on Austen's genius in portraying relationships and the foibles of human nature--in this case, the projection of our literary fantasies onto our daily experience."

—*M.M. Bennetts, author of May 1812*

Prince Tennyson

"After reading Prince Tennyson, your heart will be warmed, tears will be shed, and loved ones will be more appreciated. Jenni James has written a story that will make you believe in miracles and tender mercies from above."

—*Sheila Staley, Book Reviewer & Writer*

"Divinely inspired, beautifully written—a must read!"

—*Gerald D. Benally, author of Premonition (2013)*

"Prince Tennyson is a sweet story that will put tears in your eyes and hope in your heart at the same time."

—*Author Shanti Krishnamurty*

Jack and the Beanstalk

Jenni James

StoneHouse Ink 2013
StoneHouse Ink
Boise ID 83713
http://www.stonehouseink.net

First eBook Edition: 2013
First Paperback Edition: 2013
ISBN: 978-1-62482-061-8

Cover design by Phatpuppy Art
Layout design by Ross Burck

This book was professionally edited by Tristi Pinkston
http://www.tristipinkstonediting.blogspot.com

Published in the United States of America

This book is dedicated to Dalen, Tanner, and Carson. I love you. May your life be full of amazing adventures!

Jack and the Beanstalk

DEAR READER,

While you do not have to read Hansel and Gretel before this one—as each book is its own tale—it is best that you understand that Jack and the Beanstalk is the continuing story of Hansel and Gretel, as Jack is their son. I have included the following blurb from the back of the book so you may get a feel for the prequel and understand the circumstances.

– Jenni James

Hansel and Gretel

A HIDDEN PRINCESS AND the boy who
saves her life—

Hansel's father finds a child lost and
alone during a violent thunderstorm. After
bringing her in from the tempest, he and his
son are startled to discover that she is Gretel,
a princess of Larkein—the enemy kingdom
their own king has just destroyed. Fearful for
her life, Hansel pleads with his father to save
her. He believes they can make Gretel good by
teaching her their ways. His kindhearted father
agrees, but with great trepidation.

Ten years later, Gretel has grown into a
lovely young woman who both infuriates and
drives Hansel to distraction while he attempts
to not lose his heart to her. When the Larkein
witch comes back in the guise of a beautiful
woman and marries their father, everything is
set into a tailspin. Now they must figure out
their new stepmother's plans and prevent her
from destroying them all before it is too late.

CHAPTER ONE

"WHAT DO YOU MEAN, she is gone?" Jack asked as he whirled around on his heel, his great brown overcoat flinging about with him. "What has been done to bring her back? Has anyone even attempted to call the authorities?"

The old woman wrung her hands nervously over her pump form. "We have! There was nothing they could do. We sent for you as soon as possible."

Jack paused his pacing on the worn rug in the main cottage room of his dearest Rachel's home. "So you mean to tell me that sometime last night, Miss Rachel, *my* Miss Rachel, was taken forcefully from her bedchamber by a great beast of a man, and none of you bothered to wake me up to attend this search of her?" He was livid. He was *more* than livid. He was terrified, heartbroken, worried out of his mind. "Why, it is nearly seven o'clock in the morning! This giant monster is hours ahead of us, and I am just now hearing of it."

"We are sorry!" cried the man Jack had hoped to call a father one day. "We were not attending properly. All we could hear ringing in our minds was the memory of her screams of fright over and over again as he took her from us."

Jack was going to be sick. He swallowed and breathed deeply before attempting to speak again. "I understand this house has been under great duress the past few hours, but you must know I love your daughter more than I love my own life. I am frantic with the need to rescue her at this moment. Please, I ask that you forgive my hastiness in chastising you at such a time and instead, give me any bit of information you can so I may bring my fiancée back. Anything at all." He knelt before the older man and woman, still in their night attire with shawls and slippers. "And I vow to you both that I will not give up my search for your daughter, unlike the authorities. I will not simply hear who has captured her and run in fear. Nay, I am yours, I am hers, and you *will* see her again or I will die trying to attempt the thing."

"Oh, Jack! What would we do without you?" Mrs. Staheli clutched his hands, tugging him up. "Come and have a cup of tea and we will tell you all we know."

He shook his head. "No. I would prefer to hear it all now, just as we are, so I may begin this search instantly."

"Son, it is useless. The monster—the giant—he took her up in the clouds," her father answered as he ran his hands through his hair.

"I beg your pardon—he took her where? No, wait. Start at the beginning and tell me everything you can of this giant and all that happened. I will see what is to be done."

Celeste glanced over and shared a look with Hans.

Jack leaned toward the couple and tried his best not to let his growing irritation show upon his face as Hans cleared his throat. Why were these two moving so slowly? Every second wasted was a second he could be using to fetch Rachel back.

"It was quite late—nearly morning—when he came," Hans started.

"Yes, I know this. Why did he abduct her? Did he say?"

Celeste clutched her shawl. "Yes! Yes, that is definitely something I can answer. He wanted her voice. Apparently, his ears picked up the sound of her humming and singing the other day while she was in the meadow picking those flowers." She pointed over to a vase of wildflowers on the worn oak dining table. "He decided to bring her back to his castle so she would sing for him."

"And he also mentioned something about her playing the harp for him," Hans added.

"The harp?" Jack tried not to smile at the absurdity. "She does not do any such thing."

"So she told the giant." Hans folded his arms. "But he would not listen to her."

"Why did he not take her when he had her alone in the meadow?" Jack asked.

"He did not say."

"How did he get here? And you are certain he took her up to the sky?"

"Aye." Hans unfolded his arms and then clasped his hands together. Jack noticed the slight tremor in her as Celeste hung on to her husband's elbow. "We heard her shouts for help and came in the room immediately. The giant's huge head peered into the windows. One long arm snaked in and captured her up in his palm. She tried to make him see reason and not take her from the house. I believe he is a bit dimwitted, as each time Rachel asked him a question, it slowed him down—he would stop and think about it and then answer her. It was a clever ploy and even we joined in until he caught on to what we were doing. Then he swung his arm out and brushed us both down before wrapping his fingers around her and sliding his hand through the window again. It was a tight fit and required precision to get his fist out."

"What are some of the things he said?"

"Most of it you already know," Hans said. "He was taking her up to his kingdom in the clouds where she was meant to live in a golden cage and sing for him, or play the harp. And how he had found her in the first place."

"How did he get back up to his kingdom, and where did he come from? Has anyone heard of this giant before?"

"We had no idea he existed until he came for her." Celeste brought her hand to her mouth. "So, so terrifying."

"This is all baffling. No wonder the authorities are useless. Where does one begin? How does one get all the way up into the clouds to rescue her?"

Hans pulled away from his wife. "If you follow me outside, I can show you his tracks and where they lead. When we made it to the window and watched him take her away, it was as if the giant were climbing on something, but we could not make out what it was. Indeed, there was nothing to be seen there at all."

Jack nodded to Hans. "Let me follow you where the tracks lead. Perhaps I will find something then, something to make sense of all this."

Hans paused at the door as he pulled on his outer coat. "Celeste, we will be back shortly."

She shooed them away with her hand. "Yes, go. I could not bear to go out there again anyhow."

As the men stepped outside, Jack was amazed to see that the giant's footprints had formed six-foot craters all over the Stahelis' garden as well as the road and up a small embankment about a half mile away. They did not need to travel that far to see the great indents he left.

"Are you sure that is where they stop, up there?" Jack pointed to the hill.

"Yes." Hans turned and gestured toward the cottage. "And from that window just there—her bedroom window—we watched him make his way up an invisible rope or ladder of some sort, up into the clouds until they could not be seen anymore. It all happened so fast once he got her out of the house. We rushed to see where he was taking her. I had hopes to follow them, but he had already run here and was climbing up the thing within seconds. I have never seen anyone disappear so fast in my life. We knew it was useless to attempt to go after him."

Jack placed his hands on his hips and

shook his head, his eyes scanning the sky above them.

His father and mother, Hansel and Gretel, had warned him that life was full of adventures and that one day he would meet one that would change everything he had ever believed about himself. He sucked in a long breath of air. It would seem his particular adventure had met him after all.

There was a certain giant out there who needed to be introduced to the wrath of Jack.

CHAPTER TWO

JACK MARCHED INTO HIS home, his mind whirling with the things he must do. He had been over the entire hill where the giant's footprints ended to determine what had happened to her. The imprints in the ground did seem to imply that a sort of large, invisible item had been there, but was now gone. Whatever it was, whatever the giant had used, that was his ticket to getting Rachel back.

"Why are you in such a foul-looking mood?" asked his sister. Jill leaned back against the family's small settee with a book in her hand, her feet on the cushions.

"Have you not heard the news?" he asked, stunned that hearsay of Rachel's disappearance had not reached Jill yet.

"News? What news?" Her cotton dress brushed the wooden floor as she swung her legs down from the sofa and sat up properly. "Does it have something to do with why Mother and Father have been gone all morning?"

Jack thought of the several people who had descended upon the Staheli's cottage to be of help while he was there. The word spread so quickly that he left the place to find peace and solve this riddle himself. "Aye. I am assuming so. Though I did not see either of them, that does not mean they were not part of the crowd."

Tossing her book upon the sofa, Jill stood up. "Tell me everything. What has happened? What reports would put you in such a state?"

He ran his hands through his hair. "Rachel is gone. She was stolen." At his sister's gasp, he continued, "Her parents speak of a great giant who reached into her room last night and took her."

"And no one has tracked him and found

her yet?"

Jack was surprised to feel a chuckle escape. "They cannot. No one knows how to get to him."

"What do you mean?"

He pulled off his suddenly warm overcoat and hung it on a peg in the front closet. "He apparently has a kingdom of some sort in the sky and has taken her there."

"What? How?"

"That is something no one has been able to figure out as of yet. Though I spent quite a few hours at the last spot where he was seen this morning, it has left me baffled."

She walked up to him, her hand clutching his shirtsleeve for a moment. "Jack, you must go after her. No one will be able to figure this out but you. You are the best at solving riddles."

He reached over and held her hand. "No one else *should* figure this out but me. I am the one who must go after her."

Her blue eyes met his. He watched as a spark of life simmered deep within them. "I believe you have finally found your adventure."

"Aye. I have."

She brought her other hand up, sandwiching his hand with both of hers. "You must take me with you. You must!"

He looked at that eager face below him and smirked. "This is not something that can be considered fun and daring—this is not a lark, Jill. This is real. And one of us could die attempting to do what must be done."

She grinned. "Of course it is fun and daring! How could it not be? And you—you will more than likely solve the puzzle of the giant quicker than you realize! And we will be finding our way up to the kingdom and bringing Rachel back home very soon. I know it. I can feel it bubbling inside me. You were meant to do this—and I was meant to come along and help."

"Jill," he said with a voice of warning, "do not become overly excited. I am not convinced it would be wise to take you."

She pulled away from him. "Then you are a fool to believe you will be able to do this on your own. Two heads have always been better than one—you know this! Have not our parents taught us this every time they speak of their own tale?"

Jack walked toward the basin in the kitchen and fetched himself a cup of water from the pitcher nearby. He knew his sister had incredible sense and could reason much better than he could—usually solving dilemmas in half the time. Mayhap he was foolish to think of leaving her behind. Her defensive skills were good too, and he was a simpleton indeed to believe she could not out-master a dimwitted giant. He took another long drink and then wiped his mouth with the back of his hand. Glancing over, he saw the pout upon Jill's lips as she sat back on the settee, and attempted to appease her a bit by distracting her with one of her favorite subjects. "That witch our parents speak of was purely wicked to have thought to eat them, and ruin Grandfather as she did."

"Yes." Jill did not look up.

Goodness, she was certainly in a mood. "Well now, I did not take you for a little child," Jack said as he walked into the living area.

She folded her arms, still not meeting his eyes. "You have no right to exclude me and yet you will, simply because I am a girl."

He stepped directly in front of her, his boots touching hers. "No, you are wrong. If I would not have allowed you to go, it is because I did not want you to die. It has nothing to do with you being a girl."

"I am seventeen!" she exclaimed. "Well old enough to be considered for adventures."

"Yes, you are," he said simply. "Which is why I have decided to let you come."

She glanced up at him. "What did you say?"

He shrugged and grinned at her. "Besides, I need my navigator. Who would I turn to if I got lost?"

She laughed. "Yes, you do need me."

"Yes." He took a deep breath. "Thank you for being willing to support me."

Rolling her eyes, she stood up, causing him to move back a few paces. "Do not become all mushy and sentimental now. Let us wait until we find ourselves in that kingdom, and then you can thank me all you wish."

"We need magic. It will be the only way."

"Aye, I was thinking the same," she

muttered as she brushed past him. "Where could we even begin to look for such a thing? Who do we know with access to it? Without magic, we will by no means be able to reach that kingdom. Even though I have never heard of a giant living in the clouds, there must be someone who has."

"Yes, I believe so too. This cannot be the only time he has made his way to our land."

"So where do we go to find a person who could help us?"

"Perhaps they will come forward, now that word is out that Miss Rachel is missing."

"No!" Jill spun on her heel and turned toward him. Her face held an expression as if she had remembered something. "No! That is not the answer. We do not wait for the person to find us—we must go to the place where the magic was created. The only place we know where true enchantment lies."

Jack's gaze met hers. "You do not mean …"

Her smile beamed. "Of course I do! Where else would all the answers we seek be buried but in the Larkein kingdom?"

"Mother's castle."

"Precisely. It is the perfect place to begin looking."

"Jill?"

"Hmm?"

"You are brilliant!"

"I know." She laughed. "So are you coming or not?"

CHAPTER THREE

BY THE TIME THE two had packed their belongings and gathered up the maps and necessary food to make the trip, their parents were walking in the door.

"Pa!" Jack exclaimed. "I am so glad to see you. Jill was about to go find you both to let you know what we are planning to do, but you made it home."

"And what is this?" Gretel asked as she took off her blue knit shawl, hanging it in the front closet. "Are you two off to find this giant, then?"

Jack nodded. "Aye. We hope to—I must

do something."

Hansel shared a look with Gretel before saying, "I want you to be careful."

"I know it would be useless to tell you no when it is Miss Rachel Staheli involved," his mother said, "but for your own sakes, be safe."

"Where are you planning to go? Do you have an idea about how to reach the giant's kingdom?" his father asked.

Jill smiled. "Well, we have heard of your adventure often enough. Jack and I have figured our best chances of finding anything at all of the giant's home and how to reach it will come from your kingdom, Mother."

"Mine?" Gretel gasped. "You mean to go to Larkein?" She stepped forward and clutched Jill's hand. "Children, you do not know what evil magic resides in such a place. The castle has been dismantled and overrun for a reason. I do not wholly trust the village, either, even though it is still standing."

"But with great evil will also come the answers we seek," Jill replied.

Jack spoke up. "Mother, we have no choice. I will not allow Rachel's fate to be determined by our fears. We must go and find what we can."

"Whatever you do, do not tell them you carry the Larkein bloodline, children. Do you understand me? It has still not been long enough for people to forget all that kingdom did, and I will not have you harmed because of the folly of your heritage. Nor would I like to hear of any malicious person coming after you because of it. We are simple farmers, not heirs to any throne. Do you understand?"

Hansel took a deep breath. However, when Jack glanced over, his father remained silent.

Jill wrapped her mother up in a big hug. "It will be well. We promise not to let anyone know who we are, and we will be vigilant and we will not be attacked by any evil."

Gretel chuckled and hugged her in return. "The falsehoods you children tell just to appease your mama! I would not be surprised if your nose grew as long as Pinocchio's!"

Jill laughed. "Well, perhaps not mine. But Jack's may grow that long."

"Ha!" He smirked before turning to his father. "Pa, do you mind if I take my cow with me? She is the only thing of value I have to trade, should I need to."

Hansel nodded. "It may be wise to do so. She is not part of our herd, so will not be overly missed if you should sell her."

"Those were my thoughts exactly. Thank you."

"You must take the horse and cart and tie her to the back. There is no reason for you to attempt to walk the whole way there."

"Will you not miss them?" Jack frowned. "How will you do the work here without them?"

"Do not worry yourself over me. Miss Rachel needs you more than I need the silly horse and cart. All shall be fine—you will see."

"Well!" Jill was all smiles. "Shall we go and have our adventure, then?"

Hansel reached out and mussed up her fiery red curls. "Be careful what you wish for, little one. Always remember—adventure will find you, but it comes at a price. For it is when we least expect it that we must stand up for what we believe in and love most."

"Your father is right, children. Be brave. Be strong. But remember, this is not done on a lark, little Jill. This is done because you must—because it is right," Gretel added.

"When you find out what you must in Larkein, come back and I will see if I am able to make the trek with you to the giant's kingdom," Hansel said.

Gretel frowned. "I worry about your back. You were not as young as you once were."

"Enough, woman." He waved his hand. "I am fine. Now, let us hurry and say goodbye to these rascals so we may have them returned to us quicker."

"Do you have a tent?" Gretel stepped forward. "And enough food? Blankets? You will most likely be sleeping in the cart on the edge of the road. Find safe clearings, and remember to follow the signs. Keep off darkened paths as well."

"Mother!" Jack chuckled as he leaned forward and kissed her cheek. "We shall be fine. We have been many places and always returned to you. We are not as little as you would like us to be anymore."

"I know, I know."

Pa wrapped his arm around her shoulders

and kissed her cheek too. "She will always fret. She is your mother, after all."

"Go, before I change my mind."

Jack smiled. "Mother, you could change your mind a hundred times and it would not alter the fact that I will be going—I must go."

"Yes, you do." She sighed. "I love you."

Jill added, "Do not worry, Ma. I promise to take good care of him."

"Aye, take care to drive me nutty."

The whole group laughed and gave a final farewell of hugs.

Just before they left, Hansel slipped a few silver pieces into Jack's pocket and grasped his forearms for a moment. They exchange a long look before his father nodded. "You are ready. Bring her back."

Jack's heart swelled, the confidence in his father's eyes doing more for his sudden rush of nerves than anything ever had. "Thank you. I will."

CHAPTER FOUR

IT TOOK TWO DAYS for Jack and Jill to make their way to the Larkein village that housed the ruins of the castle. Using the silver coins his father had given him, Jack paid for a room for a night at the local inn and a few meals for their stay. After supper, when they made their way up the creaking stairs, they were pleasantly surprised to find two clean beds with a folded cloth screen separating them.

Jill had been so exhausted after a nearly sleepless night on the road that she lay upon her pillow and fell promptly to sleep. Jack, on the other hand, had noticed a group of men down in the inn's tavern and wondered if they would be a good source to ferret out some information about the enchantments in the area and, more importantly, to learn if any one of them had heard of a giant kingdom in the sky.

He tossed his bags near the small end table by his bed and changed out of his dusty outerwear into more suitable shirt and trousers for the tavern life below. As quickly as possible, he made his way down to the other men. They were a bright, cheerful group who beckoned him to sit with them as they dwindled away their hours before heading home to their womenfolk later that evening.

Jack ordered a pint of ale, though he was not sure of the brew or how strong it would be in these parts. He only pretended to sip the thing. It was about a good half hour into his chat with one of the men—Charlie, a bearded fellow looking to be in his early forties, with a bellowing voice—when an opening came up for Jack to ask about the giant. Charlie's Larkein brogue was thick and it had taken several minutes before Jack could follow the conversation enough to find the opening he needed.

"Me missus and I like to go a'walkin' out in them woods every now and then, but you gotta be keepin yer eyes on the lookout because you never know what you's bound to find in them woods. Can clean scare the hair right off yer moustache, them woods do."

Jack raised his brows. "And you took your wife out there?"

"Oh, goodness, no!" The man laughed and pounded the thick wooden table. "Nay. Me wife took *me*, she did! She likes to scare herself silly and takes me along only 'cuz it makes her laugh to see me catch fright too."

"She sounds like a brave woman indeed."

"Aye. She can outride and outshoot any man, and she's got a temper to match! She's a mean 'un!"

Jack could not imagine his sweet Rachel doing any such thing. His brows rose even more. "My word."

"Aye, she be a fine woman indeed. A very fine woman." Charlie leaned over and nudged Jack with his elbow. The smell of ale on his warmth breath assaulted Jack's nostrils. "But don't you go a lookin' at her and wantin' her for yerself! With yer pretty looks and bright gold hair, you'd be catchin her eye right quick. But she's mine there. Mine, I say."

Jack coughed, positive by the worn features of the man that his wife no doubt looked to be every bit her age. "You have nothing to worry about, sir. I am engaged to a beautiful maiden. I would not look elsewhere if a world of beauties came flocking to my door."

"A pretty speech for a pretty face, but I tells you—when you see her, you be lookin' away right quick, if you knows what's good fer ya."

Jack chuckled. "I promise, I will!"

"Good." The man grinned into his ale as he took another swig. "Anyways, as I was sayin' afore I got so sidetracked by my lovely Mary, I was a gonna tell you—since you are new to these parts—don'tcha go down any of these wooden lanes without one of us to take ya. There are a right scary bunch of fears and jumbles of nightmares in them woods. You keep yerself along the marked and well-used paths or you never know what may come and getcha."

The man had just given Jack the perfect opening to ask about the giant. Nodding, he said, "Thank you for that advice. I will surely take it." He leaned closer to the man, this time ignoring the reek of warm ale. "Have you ever heard of giant men roaming about these parts?"

"Giants?" The man pulled back and looked around the group. When he saw that no one was watching them, he hissed, "Did you say giants?"

"Yes. Have you seen one?" Jack whispered.

"Have I? My great fright!" The man slapped his hand upon the table again. "Yes, I have. And I barely escaped to tell the tale."

"Really?" Eagerly, Jack asked, "What was he doing here?"

Charlie glanced around then and fidgeted. "Aye. I probably look somethin' odd to you about now, don't I? But ye see, I can't shake this feeling that the witch is what sent him to us. And I am always uneasy at the thought of her around us and maybe hearin' right what we says."

"The witch?" Jack's stomach dropped.

"You have a witch nearby? One who lives here in Larkein?"

The man threw his head back and guffawed a long while before exclaiming, "You means to tell me you came to Larkein and you had no's notion of a witch abein' here? Are you daft? Everyone knows we's gots ourselves a witch. A downright nasty one, too!"

CHAPTER FIVE

JACK SLOWLY TURNED IN his chair to see a beautiful woman standing just within the doorway of the inn. Her long black locks curled temptingly to the waist of her green velvet gown and she looked to be no older than him. He met her striking emerald gaze; it was hooded by thick, dark lashes. Certainly, she was one of the most stunning women he had ever beheld.

Jack cleared his throat. "Forgive my manners—I did not mean to offend when I asked about you of this good man here. I had not known you existed."

She grinned, her full lips teasing him with the tilt of her smile. "Boy, you will soon learn that I do exist—very much so. In fact," she took a step toward him, "I exist so well that I even know your name and your quest, Jack Waithwrite." She raised a brow and placed a graceful hand on her hip.

He tried to hide his gulp as best as he could, but from the looks of the humored witch, it was obvious he did not succeed. "I— Well, hello," he attempted.

She smirked. "Hello yourself, boy."

"H—how do you know my name?"

As she laughed, Jack glanced at the men around him. No one would meet his eye. Indeed, not one of them would even look in his direction. She had the face of an angel, but from their reactions, she must be more wicked than he could imagine.

"Come with me, Jack. I have something I wish to show you." She held out her hand and beckoned him. "We shall go for a walk, you and I."

"Just around the stable yard?" he asked, worried to travel too far from the inn with Jill asleep upstairs.

She seemed to find his request amusing. Actually, she seemed to find every single thing about him amusing. It was a bit disconcerting.

"If you wish, I will not take you far from your fragile security." She beckoned again. "Now come."

Jack glanced back at Charlie, who briefly met his eyes with a slight shake of his head before staring into his empty mug of ale again.

Jack cleared his throat and stood up. Turning around, he met her bright emerald gaze. "Forgive me for changing my mind. I thank you for the offer, but it is getting quite late and I am tired."

A flash of irritation went across her features as she asked, "I beg your pardon? What did you say?"

"I—I was merely—"

"I know what you said, boy!" she snapped, her pretty features distorting into an ugly snarl. "I am not used to being turned down. And I certainly hope that yet another Waithwrite is not attempting to do just that." She folded her arms in front of her. "This is not up for negotiation. It was a command, Jack. You will follow me now, or you will be sorry."

How exactly did she know who he was? A cold feeling of fear went through his body. She could not possibly be Cora Childress, not after all these years. His parents killed her, did they not? His gaze traveled the length of her intricate green velvet gown. She honestly did not look a day over twenty, and she would have to be at least twice that age. When his eyes met her impatient look, he simply said, "Yes, ma'am," and followed her. What else was he to do?

"Smartly played, boy," she whispered as they walked out into the dark night.

The inn was situated next to a narrow road. To the right of the tavern were the stables and large coach house, where weary travelers could exchanges horses or rest theirs up for the night. It faced a few brick cottages nestled together across the street in front of a large wooded area. The dwindling smoke from their chimneys showed that the families had more than likely gone to bed awhile ago.

The witch did not cross the road, but stayed in the wide stable yard as she had promised. She looked intently at the moon for several moments before Jack asked, "What did you wish to show me?"

His overcoat was upstairs, and his thin jacket did not hide the chill of the night breeze. He had expected to hear her speak immediately, and found that the longer he stood next to her in silence, the more frustrated he became. "Is there something you wished to say to me, perhaps?"

She brought one hand up to halt him, her gaze still focused upwards.

After a few more moments, he tried again. "Ma'am, if there is—"

"Shh!"

Jack folded his arms and tucked the jacket closer around his frame. He could feel the beginnings of a slight shiver coming on. It would not do to catch cold just because some silly witch had decided to demand nonsense of him. He shrugged his shoulders and began to return to the inn.

"I suggest you stay put another few minutes or you will never see your dear Rachel Staheli again."

His whole body tensed before he whipped around. "Who are you?" he demanded.

She lowered her gaze and looked at him, her smirk challenging him to react badly. "Do you honestly want to know the answer to that question?"

He walked up to her. "Yes! You seem to be familiar with quite a lot about me—and I would like to know something about you. Who are you?"

Chuckling, she shook her head. "Aww… Little Jack, you should watch your temper around me. It is not wise to upset one with power." All at once, her features twisted as one long arm snaked out and clutched the lapel of his jacket. "Remember this," she hissed. "I am your worst enemy. I will always be the one who threatens your life and everything you hold dear! I nearly killed your father and mother, and I will not hesitate to destroy you."

He found himself becoming more angry the longer she spoke. "What do you want, Cora Childress?"

She blinked and seemed surprised, but did not lessen her grip on his clothing. "I need you. I need to form a sort of uneasy alliance with you."

He pulled away from her. "What do you

mean?"

"I know how to get to Rachel, but I cannot go to the giant's kingdom. I need you to do so."

"You want Rachel?" Were all of the magical beings after his beloved?

"Of course not, you fool! What would I do with her?" Cora looked back up at the moon. "No, I want the giant—or more importantly, I want the baby he stole from me. I want my Verity back! And you and your sister are the only ones who can do it."

CHAPTER SIX

JACK FELT AS IF his head were spinning. "Forgive me, but I do not understand. You had a baby? And the giant has stolen it?"

"Yes! And I want her back."

"Why would the giant steal a child?"

She rolled her eyes and spun on her heel, the skirts of her dress fanning out behind her. "Because this child has a special gift, one that must be harnessed properly or it could destroy this world as we know it."

A surprised chuckle burst from Jack. "Truly? The baby could destroy the world?"

"Yes!" She glanced back at him and then

up at the sky. "It does not matter. The giant does not know how to control her gift anyway. No one knows how she does it, and I have only seen her use it twice before."

"It must be some gift if a giant is willing to entertain a baby to have it."

"It is." Shaking her head, she continued, "But then again, being able to turn things into gold would be considered an amazing gift."

Jack ran his hand through his blond curls and whistled softly. "Indeed!"

"I want her back—now. I do not like anything that is rightfully mine to be stolen away. I found her—she is mine. I need her returned safely." Cora began to pace the gravel yard. "And you will do it for me—I saw to that."

Wait. Could he have heard her properly? "You were behind Rachel's disappearance?"

She waved away his anger. "Yes, of course. How else could I get Verity back? I needed a strong, brave lad to do it for me—a lad with Larkein blood in his veins."

"Let me make sure I understand you fully." He felt the fury within him begin to boil to new heights. "You risked the life of the woman I love. The woman I hope to marry very shortly. You have terrified her and made her completely traumatized and upset because you have a personal vendetta against a giant? And all of this you did so that I may act as your errand boy and fetch this baby for you?"

She stopped her pacing. "Yes, essentially. That is the gist of it."

"Why?" he roared, his rage filling the night.

She flinched and took a couple of paces back.

"Why would you do anything so dimwitted as to risk *my* Rachel?"

"Excuse me?" Cora put her hands on her hips.

"No!" He shook his head. "No, there is no excuse for you, ma'am! My grandfather, my father, and my mother were forced to play in your scheme, and now my sister and my dear fiancée and I find ourselves risking our lives for the same ignorant, selfish witch who nearly killed my family? Are you out of your mind?"

He walked up to her. "I know you have the power to do all sorts of things to me—I have heard the tales. I discern as well that you will most likely wish to eat me and my sister before this is all over. But I also recognize that you would not dare touch me now."

"And why not?"

He grinned. "Because unlike my father in his day, I am familiar with your weaknesses." Pulling a leather cord from within his shirt, he reached down until his fingers wrapped themselves around the small vial at the end of it and held it out to her. "I keep this on my person always. In case I will ever have use of it."

Her eyes narrowed. "Is that my potion? Where did you find that?"

Smiling, he tucked it into his shirt again. "You left quite a bit of the stuff with my grandfather."

"I would wipe that grin off your face. If you truly knew everything about me, you would know that I can freeze you at any second."

He tilted his head and shrugged, hoping it would make her angry. "Yes, I know, but you will not."

"Ha! Do not tempt me, boy. I have no use

for such flippancy."

"If you freeze me, how would I ever get to your dear golden baby? Hmm?" When she did not answer, he continued, "Rachel's parents said the giant was not very bright. Who knows how well he is taking care of the child."

Cora's eyes widened at the realization.

"I am sure he has no idea how to feed her, what to give her, how to attend her—anything."

"I am well aware of this!" she snapped. "Which is why I need you to come quickly!"

He took a deep breath and rubbed his jaw. "Two things I wish to understand at this time. First, how did you know I would come here?"

She blinked. "'Tis Larkein, the kingdom where all the magic is held. You would have to come here or you would never see your fiancée again. It is the only place with the answers you seek."

"Fair enough." He nodded, then asked, "Secondly, why can you not fetch her yourself? You are supposedly extremely magical—why have you not already done so?"

She grunted a very unladylike grunt and

spun on her heel again. "I cannot breach the contract my sisters made with the giant years ago—*centuries* ago. It is unheard of. Back when we locked him up in his skyward kingdom, we made a treaty of sorts to guarantee he would never take up residence down here again. We purposely built a castle of the finest amenities and richest luxuries for him so he would never wish to live here. And, for the most part, he leaves us alone." She began to pace once more. "Unless, of course, he gets word of children who can change things to gold—then obviously he feels it is his right to steal her. Giants are known for their treasure hoarding."

Frustrated, Jack continued, "Wait—how did the giant find Rachel? How did he know she could sing?"

Cora halted and grinned. "Oh, there are many ways to send a giant a message when one needs to. Have you not heard of creatures that can fly?"

He had never felt the desire so forcefully to strike a woman before. Taking another deep breath, he asked the next question as calmly as possible. "You sent a message telling him of her so that he might come and steal her away?"

"Yes."

"So I might become your errand boy and fetch back your baby?"

"Yes. I had watched you the last couple of days. I knew you were like your father and would go after her, no matter the cost."

"And how in all of heaven's name do you plan for me to do so?"

CHAPTER SEVEN

FINALLY. CORA HAD THE boy right where she wanted him. "It is well you have begun to see reason." She smiled. "I have a way, obviously, but I need you to give me some collateral first."

"Collateral? You are asking me to give up something of mine so I may do a favor for you? Are you mad?"

Oh, how she loved his fire. His spirit was definitely a fun challenge and something she would humor for the moment. Of course, there would be time later to make him pay for his impertinence. "Yes. It is the way all magic works. You give me something, and then I will give you the tools you need to finish your quest."

His eyes narrowed. "What would you ask for payment?"

The cow he brought would do, but it was never wise to bargain quite so low. "I will take your sister until you return with Verity."

"Never! She comes with me or this deal is off."

Cora raised an eyebrow and walked up to him, surprised he did not flinch. Looking him over from head to toe, she smirked. "No, I see that you will need one as smart as she is to keep you safe." Placing her hand on her hip, she pretended to think it over. "The vial?" she asked.

"You wish to take my only defense?" He shook his head. "No."

"Yes, you are wise to hold on to that. It may be very useful against the giant." She sighed and then said, "What do you have that you are willing to part with?"

"A very fine cow that you may keep forever."

She laughed. "Your fiancée's life depends

on me taking your old dried-up cow? Are *you* mad?"

"She is not old, or dried up! In fact, her milk is so rich it is nearly cream."

Even better. Good, thick milk was the main ingredient in many of her spells. "Very well. I will trade you the cow for these." She carefully pulled out a small leather drawstring pouch from her waistband and allowed the three items to fall into the palm of her hand.

"What are they?" Jack leaned over. "They look like beans."

"They are."

"This is preposterous! Are you mocking me? I will not trade my cow for three measly beans. Take them away."

Folding her fingers over them, she shrugged and pretended nonchalance. "Very well." Turning as if she was about to leave, she said over her shoulder, "I wish you luck in finding your Rachel without them." With that, Cora began to walk past the stables and out toward the road, and then counted the seconds it would take for him to stop her.

One.

Two.

Three.

Four.

Five.

Six.

Sev—

"Halt!" he called out.

Grinning, she paused and waited for him to catch up.

"Why would you give me beans? Are they magical?"

"Of course!" She would laugh if the question were not so stupid.

"What should I do with them?"

She held out her hand and set the beans on his palm. "You plant them. Give them a little love and some water, and you will be amazed at what you find. Though, plant them somewhere far from the house."

"But what will they do?"

"Why, grow, of course. What did you expect?"

He let out a frustrated sigh. "So, you are telling me that these beans will grow. And somehow, someway, they will then lead me to the giant? When I eat the vegetable, will I sprout wings to help me fly up there, or will they provide another way equally as absurd?"

"You will just need to plant them and see."

He brought his hand up into the moonlight. "These look like very ordinary beans to me. How do I know you are not pulling the wool over my eyes and planning to make off with my cow?"

Smirking, she replied, "You do not. You must learn to trust that perhaps all I have said is correct and I am not mocking you or leading you on a merry chase."

Jack shook his head. "I have no reason to trust you—none—and every single reason to believe you are a thief, an imposter, and a liar."

"Then you *are* in a pickle, are you not?"

"Honestly!" He threw his arms in the air, his fist tight around the beans. "This is the help you give me? You want me to save your baby and my fiancée with nothing but a few beans, and I am supposed to believe they will miraculously bring the girls back?"

"No. I never said that." Her gaze met his. "I do not promise that you will be able to bring either of them back. I have only given you the means to get there. The rest is up to you—if you are willing to trust a wicked witch, of course." She chuckled, keeping the conversation light. But her heart beat wildly, hoping she did not err in her judgment of him. She needed that child!

"I have no choice, do I?" He looked away.

"Everything worth living for requires sacrifice. Those things we love most do not come free. Magic needs a certain willingness, faith, and bravery to do all it requires for it to come about. I could tell you exactly what those beans would do—but then it would negate your ability to prove your faith. Even so, I gave you the greatest and easiest way to get to the giant's kingdom. And when you use the beans and fully understand their power, then what? Then courage steps into play, and you may not be brave enough to do what you must to get the girls back."

She continued. "I, too, am risking a lot. Those three beans are all I have left. If I have handed them to the wrong person, I need to know now."

"Are they truly worth that much to you?"

As if she would stand here in the cold

night air negotiating with a lad of twenty if they were not. "Those beans are worth more than sixty of the finest cows in the kingdom!" she hissed. "Mark my words, boy. I am not here to fool about. I will only exchange them for Verity's safety. If you do not mean to believe me, I will take back what is mine and finish this deal now. Are you, or are you not, willing to sacrifice for the love of your life, or is this all simply a game of heroics you decided to play?"

"Yes." He took a deep breath. "Very well, I will exchange the cow for the beans."

"Good." She snapped her fingers and grinned at the surprise on his face when the cow appeared before them. "You and your father do not know all I can do. Think over what I have just said. For a long while, he has believed me burned within a cottage. I did not die, did I?" She raised an eyebrow. "Besides, even a witch can learn a few tricks after all these years." She tugged on the collar of the cow and smiled. "Good luck. I will be watching you."

And then she disappeared before him in a puff of smoke.

CHAPTER EIGHT

JILL AWOKE TO THE sound of Jack coming
into the room. "Are you finally here?" she
asked through the screen separating their beds.
She had woken up earlier to find him gone and
figured he went out to gather information.

"Yes," he muttered. She heard his boots
as he tugged them off and they clomped to the
wooden floor.

She turned over onto her elbow. "Did you
find out anything? Will we be able to get to
the kingdom?"

"Ugh," he grunted. "I will tell you in the
morning."

"What does that mean?"

"It means I am not sure if I have just made the stupidest mistake of my life, or the smartest choice."

Her stomach clenched, and a feeling of dread came over her. "Jack, what did you do?"

There were the sounds of movement and creaking as he climbed into bed. He sighed and then said, "I bargained with a witch."

"What?" She sat up. "You did *what*?" How could he be so foolish?

"In exchange for the cow, she gave me some magic beans that are supposed to get us up to the giant in some way."

"Oh, good great mercy." Jill lay back with a plop, staring up at the darkened wood-beamed ceiling. "Do you mean to say you are not sure if the beans even work? And now the cow is gone?"

"Aye."

She harrumphed and brought the blankets up tighter.

"It gets worse."

"How can it get worse than you bargaining with a witch in exchange for mere beans?"

"The witch is Cora Childress."

JILL STILL MARVELED AT the insanity her brother had shown in confronting that witch. She held the beans in her petticoat pocket for safekeeping as they drove the cart home, but honestly could not fathom what made them so special. "Are you certain they are magic beans?" she asked for at least the twentieth time since leaving the inn. "And are you positive it was Cora Childress who gave them to you?"

"Yes and yes. Now stop asking me the same questions over and over again." He sighed and slapped the reins to bring the horse to a nice trot. They had just come to a long stretch of smooth road and now that the cow was not behind them, slowing down the journey, he let the horse have at it.

"I am sorry. I do not mean to be quite so judgmental, but what else am I supposed to think?" She readjusted herself on the hard seat and looked out at the rolling countryside. It was strikingly beautiful now that they were away from the wooded area and could actually see the lush green all around them. "When do you imagine we will be home?"

"Just before nightfall, in a few hours or so."

"Do you want to go home? Or would you rather not?"

He glanced over. "And do what? Jill, I have to plant these beans and then wait to see what happens."

"Yes, but you said it had to be done away from the cottage. Would you rather go straight to the spot, while the light is still fading, or wait until morning?"

"Oh, I might as well go tonight. I already know the field to use. The empty one in the back."

"Oh, Grandfather's field?"

"Aye."

She nodded. "So tell me about Cora. Pa says she was extremely beautiful. She must be much older now—is she still attractive?"

"I do not think she has aged a day since she ate that woman all those years ago."

Jill groaned.

"Precisely. But yes, she is a very stunning woman—so much so, I did not know what to make of her when she first addressed me."

"Jack, should we tell Father and Mother that she is not dead, or do we leave well enough alone?"

"I do not know. I have been pondering the same issue this whole day. If we tell them that not only is she alive, but she knows of our family and we are her pawns once again, I do not believe Father will take it well."

"Yes, he will most likely go after her."

"Let us wait until it is absolutely necessary to tell them. The thought of us going to Larkein must have frightened them enough."

"Not to mention the notion of us flying our way up to the giant's kingdom."

"Yes, no reason to worry them more with the knowledge that it was all orchestrated by their old foe."

Jill chuckled. "Only in our family would such things happen. What is the likelihood of any of the other villagers facing such bizarre circumstances?"

He grinned and glanced down at her. "'Tis true. We are quite the adventure seekers, are we not?"

"Then again, we do have a Larkein queen for a mother—with the magic in that kingdom, it was bound to happen."

THE SUN HAD JUST gone down as they rolled into the family's shared drive. Jack turned the horse toward Grandfather's property at the fork and then rumbled the cart along the lane until he came to the closest spot to the outer field.

He jumped down and tossed the reins into the cart before holding his arms out for Jill. Scooping her up, he quickly set her boots on the dirt before the two climbed over the wooden fence and out into the field overgrown with blooming wildflowers. The fragrant scents wafted lazily through the air as the sunset breeze rolled in. It looked to be a pleasantly warm summer's night.

Jill followed Jack as he made his way up to the crest of the little rise in the center of the field. "Why do you think we had to plant these beans so far away from the house?" She pulled them out of her pocket.

He shrugged and knelt on the grass.

Pulling up a few flowers by the roots, he soon cleared a small section.

"Do you need help?" she asked as she handed the beans to him.

He glanced up. "Actually, I need some water." Nodding toward their grandfather's cottage, he said, "Do you mind running to the outside pump and fetching a pail of water for me?"

"Do you need a lot?"

"Nay. I would imagine just a few cupfuls, really."

"I will try not to disturb Grandfather as well."

"Aye, no reason to worry him over what we are doing out here."

She scampered down the little rise and then slowed a bit as she crept closer to the cottage. It took no time at all to pump a few bursts of the well water into the small pail set near the pump. Carefully she made her way back up to Jack and handed him the bucket.

He had already put the little beans into the ground. She watched as he covered them with earth and patted it firmly. "Well, I guess we shall hope for the best."

He poured the water over the dirt mound while Jill said a silent prayer. *Please, whatever happens, let him be able to save Rachel.* When he was through, they both headed down the knoll to return the bucket.

All at once, they heard a loud roaring. The ground beneath them began to rumble and the small rise started to grow into a hill. What was happening? Jill shrieked as she watched Jack stumble and fall down. The great quaking caused her footing to slip and soon she was tumbling down the growing hill after him.

CHAPTER NINE

"JACK! JACK!" JILL SHOUTED
somewhere to the left of him.

He groaned and sat up. What had
happened? He tried to stand, but winced and
held his head. It was throbbing. He must have
hit it when he fell.

"Jack!" Her blurry figure came up to him.

What was wrong with his eyes? Why
could he not see? "What?" he asked as he
attempted to rub the pain away. Indeed, his
head hurt so much, it was as if it had split in
two.

"You are bleeding!" She gasped.

"Am I?" Bringing his hand forward, he tried to focus on it. His vision was too blurred to see blood of any kind.

"Let me assist you." He heard a tear of fabric, and then felt Jill place the cloth against his brow. "Hold this for a few minutes until the bleeding stops," she said. "I do not know why you were clutching the back of your head when it is the front that has plainly received the most damage. It was a nasty fall. Are you well?"

"Um…" He chuckled and then grimaced. "I should not laugh—it hurts. But no, I am not up to snuff."

"Well, clearly you are not all that sound, I can see that. What I meant was, is anything else damaged? Your ankles? Back? Arms?"

"Only my head." He held out a fuzzy hand to her. "I will be fine. Can you help me up? I want to turn around and see what has occurred."

"No, no, you do not. Your mind cannot fathom what is behind you at the moment. Just stay down a bit longer."

He attempted to rise again. "Jill, do not take me for a fool. What is it?" This time when he looked at her, she was more clear. He blinked. Her face came into focus. She was looking past him and up toward the sky. "What?" Turning around slowly, one hand keeping the makeshift bandage in place, he faced the most bizarre sight he had ever seen. "My word!" he whispered.

"I know." Jill sat down beside him. "It is rather magnificent, is it not?"

His eyes followed the massive green twisted tubes from the ground all the way up until he could not see them end for the clouds. "What in the world is it?"

"I do not know."

Grunting a bit, he regained his footing and walked up to the thing. He reached for a large leaf that had wound around one of the bulky tubes.

"Jack! Jill! What in all of glories be is this in the garden?" Their mother came running up the hill. "We heard the commotion and felt the quaking. Your father and I looked out the window and nearly fainted. What a sight this is!"

Hansel climbed up behind her. "Have you ever seen such a large beanstalk in your life?"

He turned to Jack and Jill. "Where did you get the beans to create this?"

"This is perfect!" His mother laughed. "What an easy way to climb up to the giant's kingdom!"

It had not hit Jack until his mother spoke that this was what the witch meant. "It is my way up there! I cannot believe it! Those silly little beans worked!"

"And quite quickly, too," Jill exclaimed.

"Jack!" Gretel gasped. "What has happened to your head?"

He brushed her hand aside. "It is fine. Just a scratch—I do not even feel a thing anymore."

"What in all the blazes is this?"

The group turned and watched Adale make his way up the hill. "What have you all been doing to my garden? I was just heading to my bed when the ground began to move and I heard this ruckus. I had to come out and see for myself."

"Forgive us," Jill said. "In exchange for a cow, we were given magic beans to fetch Rachel back. We had no idea what would happen, only that we had to bury them away from the house."

"'Tis a good thing you did!" their grandfather replied. "Just this mound of dirt alone would have been the ruin of my foundation. The whole house would have tumbled to the ground."

Jack glanced over at Jill and asked, "Are you ready to head up?"

"Now?" Her eyes traveled the length of the stalk again. "You want to go right *now*?"

"It is as good a time as any. Why not?"

Gretel walked over to him. "No, you will wait until morning before either of you traipse up any magical beanstalks. I want you both rested."

Why could she not see the importance of leaving at once? "Every second wasted on sleep will be a second Rachel is terrified and alone. I must go."

"Jack," his father replied, "your mother is right. You and Jill have taken one journey already. We do not need either of you falling because you were not fully prepared for the rigorous climb ahead of you. It is wiser to sleep first and start in the morning."

"Besides, then we can travel in daylight."

Jill placed her hand on his arm. "I know you want Rachel. I know it is more than likely killing you to stand here and be told you cannot go until tomorrow when a way to save her is before you—a way you did not think possible even ten minutes ago. But, Jack, they are wise. Please, let us wait."

He looked down at her and sighed. "You too?"

She nodded, her deep brown eyes pleading with him. Jack looked up at the stalk and weighed his options. If he went ahead, Jill would most definitely come with him. No matter how many times he told her not to, she would. And though he had the stamina and drive to get up that stalk, she would most likely fall. If he waited until they were all in bed and slipped out, she would follow him up that stalk hours later and then be lost in the kingdom. He sighed again. This was going to be a long night. How would he sleep, knowing Rachel was just a climb away? And how long would the beanstalk last?

"You do not want to wait, do you?" whispered Jill.

"No. I cannot risk it. This grew so fast—

what if we awoke and it was gone? Then we would never save her."

Hansel and Gretel exchanged looks with Adale and he spoke up. "I say let them have their adventure. They are young and will be fine. The moon is large and bright and will be enough light for them. And what Jack says is true—magic spells are tricky things. This stalk could be here for centuries or a mere twenty-four hours. One never knows."

"Right, then." Gretel stepped away. "I say we get you some more provisions and supplies and let you begin your journey now. Just promise me, you two, that you will sleep on the stalk if you become too tired. I am sure there are places to nestle safely. There is no reason to push yourselves and fall."

Jack looked at his sister. "What say you? Can I not convince you to change your mind?"

Her gaze followed the stalk and then she grinned, game as ever. "I say it is time to bring Rachel home!"

CHAPTER TEN

RACHEL LILY STAHELI OPENED her eyes
and squinted in the moonlight that streamed
through the window of the giant's castle. It
was nearly a full moon. She sat up in her bed
in the large birdcage and wrapped her arms
around her legs. How will anyone find me
way up here?

She wondered for the thousandth time
what Jack was doing and if she would ever see
him again. It was only the fourth night since
the giant had stolen her away from her home,
but it seemed she had been there a century.

She tried to stay positive, telling herself

over and over again that Jack would come for her. Even if it was impossible, he would still come. It was the only hope she had left—the thought of him caring enough to find her.

How she loved him. She missed him so very much.

Resting her head upon her knees, she turned and looked at the bright, round moon before her. Up here, as high as she was, she could make out the stars and the moon so much better than in the village below. Seeing the large orb so full and bright reminded her of the night Jack had proclaimed his love for her under the stars.

Grinning, she wiped away a silly tear. How perfectly adorable he was then. She giggled as she recalled the proper hat and suit he wore as he swept a regal bow and lowered himself to one knee. It had not occurred to her what he was about to say. Truly, it was remarkable that someone as handsome and brave and wonderful as he was could love her!

And yet, he did.

Oh, how sweet were the surprising words that left his lips! How simply glorious to hear of his love and devotion and admiration of her.

Jack. Jack Waithwrite loved her more than
any other girl. He was hers.

Urgh. She dashed at another tear as it
crawled its way down her cheek. Jack was
her rock. She had not known she needed such
a strong, steady force in her life until he was
there. And then, all at once, the pressures and
insecurities and worries and challenges did
not seem so hard to bear anymore. Indeed, he
lightened every load she carried just by being
there.

How she missed him! She worried she
would never see his handsome, smiling face
again. It was foolish to be so in love. She
knew this, knew how it could cripple someone
and make them sink into despair when their
significant other was not around. Had not her
own mother turned into a simpering water pot
every time her father went away to the grand
market?

She took a deep breath and sat up. No.
She had to be strong. Rubbing her eyes, she
pressed her lips together and looked around
the room below her. Her cage was placed at
the top of a high shelf. Never had she seen
such beauty and wealth before. The giant

might be a simpleton, but he certainly had very fine taste.

Yards and yards of lush velvet adorned the walls and furniture of the castle in deep blues and maroons and emeralds. There was not a surface or item that was not bedecked in some way. And the gold! She had never seen so much gold in all her life. Even this birdcage was made of beautiful gold filigree.

There was a soft stirring sound. She quickly glanced at the oversized music box that held the sleeping baby near her bed. The little angel with a head full of brown curls turned within her covers and sucked her thumb as she drifted back to sleep. Why in the world the giant would think to capture such a small child, she would never know.

Her hands shook slightly as she thought of the poor thing—traumatized and crying nonstop when Rachel had first gotten there. It had looked as if the giant had not fed her properly, aside from a large, stale cracker she had been gnawing on, or changed her underclothes once.

He placed Rachel in the cage with the small girl and simply said, "Fix her."

She immediately went to the baby and caught her up in her arms. The soiled clothing reeked, but the child needed comfort more than anything else. "I must be given warm water and something to bathe her in. She needs milk and proper food. She is starving and dirty. I will need clean garments for her as well."

"No, *you* fix her," said the giant as he looked in the cage at them both.

"No!" Rachel stomped her foot. "You are a bad man! You will kill this baby. Fetch me these things so I can help her."

"Gleeflak not bad man. I good man."

Rachel shook her head and remained firm. "No. You have stolen a baby and stolen me. That is bad. I need help to take care of her. It is your responsibility to see that we are cared for—both of us!"

"I not steal you. You are mine!"

"No, I am not. And I do not know where you got this baby, but thank goodness I am here or she certainly would have died. Do you want her to die?"

When he shook his head, she said, "I will fix this child, but you must do as I say. Now."

He tilted his head and grumbled a bit. "Fine. I do it. I bring you clothes and water and milk and food. But you—" He pointed right at her with one large finger through the cage. "*You* will fix her!"

"Yes." Rachel nodded as she brought the child in closer. "Yes, I will fix this baby. I promise. Now get those things before she becomes ill."

When he was gone, Rachel had pulled the whimpering child away to get a better look at her. "There you go, little one. I am here now. You do not have to be frightened anymore. All will be well." Her little legs had wrapped themselves around Rachel's waist, and the big brown eyes had stopped crying long enough to stare up at her in wonder. The child looked to be nearly two. Too young to be on her own, neglected in a cage. Rachel's heart twisted as she held the darling close to her again. "How long have you been here, little one? How frightened have you been without your mother?" The baby burst into tears, and Rachel bounced her softly in her arms. "Shh… I am here now. I will not leave you. You are safe. You have no reason to be frightened again."

Now staring at the sweet cherub all nestled in her bed with clean clothes, having contented dreams, Rachel vowed, "I will not accept our fate. Your mother must be worried sick, as sick as my family is. We will get home. I do not know how or when, but I promise you, I will get us out of here together."

CHAPTER ELEVEN

JACK HEAVED HIS WEIGHT up the next twisted vine and then leaned down to clutch Jill's hand and bring her up. "How are you doing?" he asked as she gained her footing and panted against the stalk. They had been climbing continuously, with several short breaks, for over five hours now. "Do you need to rest again?"

She looked down at the distance they had come. "It is so very far away."

"Aye," he said as he glanced at the tiny homes dotting the land below them in the moonlight. They were too high up to see their cottage or Grandfather's, but they could make out their village and several others tucked within the shadows of the rolling hills.

"How much farther do we have to go?"

Her breathing was more labored the higher they traveled. His felt off too, but it seemed to affect her much more. "I assume another hour or so."

She nodded as she continued to pant.

Even though he felt energized and willing to go on, her actions gave him pause. She needed rest—nay, she needed sleep. He glanced around the large collection of intertwined vines and found a nice outcropping that could support them both a little ways above them.

"There," he said as he pointed upwards. "Do you see that grouping of vines?"

"Yes."

"That is where I think we will take a break and sleep for the rest of the night. I am exhausted." He looked down at her weary features. "What say you?"

She heaved several more breaths before nodding.

He grinned. "Very well. Let us get you

up there, and perhaps have some food as well."

"No." She shook her head. "No food, just sleep."

"Yes, ma'am."

Grasping the strong vine next to him, he grunted as he hauled himself up. When they had begun this trek, Jill had been so quick, he was hard-pressed to keep up with her. But now, he leaned down and clutched her hand again. Tugging, he brought her exhausted body up the few more feet to the outcropping. Jill was as done as she had ever been. "There you go. Take off your pack and undo the ties of your skirts so you are more comfortable and find a nice spot where you can curl up," he commanded.

She muttered something in reply and did just as he insisted.

Chuckling, he watched her wrap herself up into a nice, cozy ball and almost instantly fall asleep, snuggled between a low-dipped thatch of vines and a large leaf blanket. He had never seen her quite so obedient before. It was good for her.

Shucking off his own pack, he brought it round and pulled out an apple and a nice-sized chunk of cheese wrapped in paper. Munching, so far above everything else, he looked out at the world and smiled. Almost. He was almost there.

Tomorrow the real journey would commence.

Hopefully all was well with Rachel. He could not envision anything but happy thoughts when it came to her predicament. Anything less than absolutely perfect imaginings would set him reeling. There was one goal and one goal only—to see that she made it home as safely and as quickly as possible. The rest of the little insecurities that crept up at the thought of him traversing through an unknown kingdom, facing larger-than-life human forms—those did not matter now. It was useless to worry about things he knew nothing about. Instead, he focused on holding her in his arms again, smelling her sweet lavender scent as he pressed his nose into her glorious pale hair and then bending down and kissing her lips softly.

He missed her.

"Rachel, I am coming. Do not give up on me. Do not wallow in despair, believing it is impossible. Nothing is impossible when you love someone as much as I love you. We will be together shortly. Just a few more hours now and all shall be well again, I promise."

He leaned back against the vines and wrapped a leaf about him. Closing his eyes, he grinned and allowed the cool breeze to carry his troubles away as he drifted to sleep.

THE NEXT MORNING DAWNED bright and clear. Jill stretched and moaned softly. Every place upon her person ached. The rigorous climb was using parts of her that had never been expanded or worked before. It was a bit disconcerting to wake up so high in the sky. "This must be what a bird feels like," she mumbled as she glanced around for Jack.

Spying him, she grinned. His mouth hung open with a small dribble of saliva trickling onto his shirt. Sitting against the vine with his head lolled to the side certainly made for an interesting look. Perhaps it was a very good thing Rachel was not here to witness this. Giggling softly to herself, Jill found her pack and, rummaging through it, quickly broke

off a piece of bread. After taking a few bites
herself, she ripped smaller bits and tossed
several Jack's way, hoping to land one in his
mouth. After many close attempts, she finally
got a piece all the way in.

"Yes!" She laughed when he spat and sat
up.

"What are you on about?" he asked as he
wiped the spittle from his chin and neck, his
eyes taking in about twenty bread pieces all
over his chest and lap. "What is this? What
have you been up to?" He gathered a few up
and plopped them in his mouth.

"Nothing." She grinned. "You just looked
so charming asleep, I had to, uh…"

Jack's eyes sparkled. "I will get you back,
wretch. You watch me."

She waggled her brows and laughed some
more. "Yes, but it was worth it to see you in
such a state. Truly, I think even Rachel herself
would be enamored with this." She leaned
back and imitated him, her mouth open and
awkward as her head lolled to the side.

Laughing, he gathered a few more of the
bread pieces and chucked them at her. "You
are a monster!"

"Yes, but you love me anyway. Now, hurry up and eat so that we may get there. My word, you are such a slugabed! I cannot believe how long I have had to wait upon you to wake up."

"Me?" He looked astonished, which only caused her to laugh more. "I am the slugabed, when you are the whole reason we had to stop to begin with? Ha."

"Goodness. The amount of time it takes you to argue about this or that and we could have been gone by now."

He shook his head and stood up. "Point taken. Let us get off this thing and go to that kingdom."

CHAPTER TWELVE

BY THE TIME JACK had reached the top
of the stalk and climbed on the ground, only
about a quarter of an hour had passed. "We
were much closer than I realized," he said as
he helped Jill step onto the grassy slope.

"It is stunning!" she gasped.

It was a very beautiful kingdom. The
castle itself was a massive fortress rising up
above them—larger than anything they had
ever seen before. It looked to be about six or
seven miles away, by their reckoning. There
were a few well-worn paths leading to the
great palace, but Jack felt it was better to be

just off to the side of the one closest, hidden in the grass, so as not to attract attention. The witch had only mentioned the one giant, but if there were more, he needed to be doubly sure they were safe.

Everything about this place was larger than life. The trees, the flowers, the cows and sheep they had seen in the distance— everything. It was certainly a different feeling to be walking amongst ordinary things and feel as though he had shrunk significantly.

"This is by far the most incredible adventure we have ever had!" Jill exclaimed as she walked under a large grouping of tulips. "I am so small, I feel like a fairy."

They pushed against the fronds and grass for a few more minutes before Jack became irritated. "Come, we must hurry," he said as he stepped out of the tall grass back onto the road. "It is too hard to traverse through that jungle. Let us stay here along the edge, but we must move fast."

Thankfully they made it to the castle without mishap. Jack guided them through the slots of the gates as they entered the main stone courtyard. The whole castle was laid out around the center open area. The three sections were all interconnected, but had several doors leading into each one. It was a beautiful fortress. The windows were tall with many panes, the carved wooden doors had gold detailing inlaid with painted flowers and motifs, and the towers held majestic red-and-gold flags that flew proudly in the breeze.

"Where do we head first?" asked Jill.

"I am not certain."

She pointed to a taller building on her left. "Well, that section looks like the chapel. See the stained-glass windows? So I would think either the section straight ahead or to the one to right."

"Then we will head straight first, and then go to the right as we begin looking for her. Remember, her parents mentioned she would most likely be in a cage of some sort. I imagine she would be in the main living rooms or the giant's own chambers, though I hope for her sake she is out in the living area."

Jill cringed. "Me too. Can you envision how awful and loud his snoring must be?"

"How many giants have you met?" Jack grinned as they began to head toward the nearest door, keeping in the shadows and away from the interior of the court.

"None."

"Then how do you know he snores?"

She nudged him with her elbow and ran ahead. "Must you continuously harass me? You yourself said that you hoped she was not in his chambers, and now you mock me for expanding on the reasons why. Great heavens, you will never let up, will you?"

"Never," he called as he caught up to her.

"How do we get in?"

They looked up at the great door. It was shut tight and appeared too heavy for either of them to open, if Jack could ever reach the handle in the first place. Glancing around, he found a door opened wide enough to let in some breeze several feet away. "There!" He pointed and then started making his way, keeping in the shadows and near the pillars, over to the door.

"You are a genius," she called after him as she followed.

"I know. Hush, now," he whispered. "If a door is ajar, it means someone is in there." They crept up to the opening and Jack stepped inside. It took a moment to adjust to the darkness of the room. He blinked several times as he attempted to make out the large furnishings around him. It was indeed a very nice room, decorated with the finest taste and style. He heard a loud snort and quickly held out his hand as Jill bumped into him. *Wait*, he mouthed, scanning the room to find the source of the noise.

"What?" she whispered.

My word, there were days when Jill acted too much a female to be considered rational. He turned toward her and mouthed again. *Be silent!*

She rolled her eyes, but thankfully did not say another word.

There was another loud snort, and this time Jack heard a rustling of some kind to the right of them. Glancing over, he caught movement from a hefty boot fully Jack's height.

Jill gasped and he knew she had seen it too. "What are we going to do?" she asked.

He turned and placed his hand over her mouth before dragging her back outside. "Jill," he fiercely whispered, "we are both going to be the giant's meal if you do not keep your mouth shut. If you cannot control yourself, stay outside. Go back to the beanstalk and wait for me there. I must find Rachel, and I cannot do so with you announcing our presence every few seconds!"

"You are such a boor!" she said once she pulled away. "I was speaking quietly enough."

"No, you were not!"

"Hey!"came a loud voice from within the room. "Who is out there making noise?"

CHAPTER THIRTEEN

"RUN!" JACK PUSHED JILL away from the door. "Hide! Go!"

"Jack?" She looked at him, but he would not budge.

They could feel the vibrating footsteps of the giant. "Fe, fi, fo, fum! Who is outside my door? Whoever they be, I do come!"

"Run!" He shouted this time, not even trying to soften his voice. "He knows someone is here. I will stay and meet his wrath. Leave so you can save us!"

Satisfied, he watch Jill run and hide behind a pillar a short distance away.

"You!" The giant's loud voice caused Jack's ears to ring. The large man bent over, his hands on his knees, peering right at him.

"Me!" Jack smiled and stood up tall, his gaze taking in the man's rather pleasant features. Why, he did not look very terrifying at all.

The giant blinked. "What you want? Who are you?"

"I am Jack Waithwrite, and I have come to be at your service." His teeth clenched behind his tight smile.

"My servant? I don't need no servant." The giant reached down and picked Jack up, squeezing his shoulders painfully.

"No? Are you sure? I would be happy to do anything you wished."

The giant looked around. "Hey, where you come from, anyway? How you find me?"

"Uh…" This was definitely not a question he could answer. If he mentioned the beanstalk, the giant might have it removed. If he mentioned the witch, the giant would know he had come for the baby. Instead, he tried a different approach. "You are a very nice-looking person. What is your name?"

The giant smiled, showing teeth that were surprisingly clean and straight. "I Gleeflak."

"Hello, Gleeflak. It is nice to meet you." Jack tried not to grimace as the large man laughed and squeezed a bit more firmly.

"Are you my friend?" Gleeflak asked.

"Uh, yes." Jack's smile felt strained.

"Good! I like friends. I always wanted a friend. Want to come sit with me? We could watch my pretty singing girl."

Relief poured over Jack. She was here. She was safe. "Yes! I would love to do that."

"Good." The giant swung his arms as he walked, most likely forgetting he had a new friend in his hand.

Jack swayed back and forth like tossing on a sea-churned ship. He was going to be ill if Gleeflak did not stop soon. He swallowed a moan, but then shouted when the giant loosened his fingers and his hold on him. As quickly as possible, Jack clung to the man's shirtsleeve and then swung his legs over his wrist as if he were riding a horse. The motive for the release was explained as soon as he saw the intricately designed cage.

Gleeflak must not be able to process more

than one thought at a time, and right now that thought was to get the singing maiden. Jack hung on as the giant brought his arm up and unlocked the clasp on the cage.

And there she was—the first time he had seen Rachel in five days. He had never glimpsed anything more perfect than she was right then. She smiled wide. Just as she was about to exclaim her joy, he shook his head and tried to convey the message not to let the giant know they were acquainted.

Rachel's brow furrowed for a second as she glanced from Jack to the giant and then back at Jack.

He winked.

And then she grinned the most adorable grin.

"Here, little singer. You come and sing to me and my friend Jack," Gleeflak said as he reached in and tugged her close to Jack. They stared at one another, Jack's gaze going hungrily all over hers, deciding which part he would love to kiss first. Her lips, that dainty nose, her bright eyes, those smiling cheeks…

"Hey, Jack? Where you go?" asked the giant, his head going back and forth. "Did I drop you?"

"No. I am here on your sleeve."

Gleeflak gave out a quick laugh. "Oh, good thing you are so fast! You are a good friend to have."

"'Tis nothing to worry over. I am quite happy where I am." He winked at Rachel again and she blushed in response. Oh, goodness, what a relief it was to be this close to her, to see her so cheerful as well.

"Gleeflak," she called up to him. "Please shut the cage so the baby does not get out."

It was then that Jack noticed the pretty little girl staring up at them from next to a music box.

Rachel turned her head toward the little girl. "I will back in just a little bit. You play with your toys and I will come for you." The baby began to pout, looking as though she were ready to cry. "Uh-uh," Rachel said. "No. You will be a happy girl and play nice. I have to go, but I will be back very, very soon, I promise." She then looked up at the giant again. "Gleeflak, could you perhaps bring the cage with us so I can see that she is all right? Truly, she is too young to leave alone all the time. It is much better for her to come with us—then she can be involved and content."

He sighed and nodded. "Fine. I help baby." With his other hand he locked the cage and picked it up. Jack could tell he was careful to remember not to drop his arms this time, holding them out as steady as possible. He was most likely on special alert because Rachel was such a novelty for him.

As the giant walked, holding the birdcage with his left hand and Rachel in his right with Jack straddling that wrist, Jack leaned over and caught Rachel's hand, lacing his fingers through hers.

"I have missed you," she whispered.

"Have you now?" He chuckled softly.

"Yes."

"I have missed you too."

She sighed and bit her lip, looking up at him with the most glorious sparkling hazel eyes. "Thank you for coming for me."

He squeezed her hand, his thumb drawing a lazy circle on her palm as they bounced to the rhythm of the giant's steps. "I would always have come for you. Always."

She nodded, and he could tell she was

blinking back tears. "I know—just thank you. I cannot imagine how you made it here, but I am so glad you did."

"Hush. I shall tell you all shortly." He glanced up at the oblivious giant and then back her way. "But for now, it is my pleasure to hear you sing again."

"I will sing it all for you. Every song. Every breath. Every—"

The giant jostled them as he set Rachel down on the table in the grand dining room. Then he walked over to a seat not too far from her and placed Jack, and then the cage, on the table next to him. "There you go. Sing. Make it good. I want my friend to see what a pretty singer you are."

CHAPTER FOURTEEN

RACHEL SMILED AT JACK and took a deep breath before beginning the song she sang particularly for him whenever he asked for it. It was a dear love song about a village maiden and a young king who loved her. A man who was hailed as the wisest in the land had chosen her over all else. He told his secrets to her—she was the one he loved. He had seen her great worth long before any of the other village lads had. It was such a beautiful song, with lilting lyrics and a sweet melody.

Today was no different than before. She sang it for him as she always had. It was

their song. She was thrilled to see that Jack
did not disguise the warm glow about him or
the enduring grin he gave just for her as she
allowed the song to weave its magic around
his heart. How she loved him. She truly could
not wait until they were together always.

Once she was done, she waited until Jack
had finished clapping before beginning another
love song.

"No!" Gleeflak shouted unexpectedly.
"Stop! Why you sing these boring songs? No.
Sing the songs I like and leave off these ones.
I don't like 'em. And you sound bad. Just so
very bad."

"You do not like my singing?"

"No! Not that singing. Sing something
else."

Rachel shared a look with Jack before
searching for a song she felt was suitable. Was
there a particular song the giant requested
more often than not? Nay, there was none. It
was always she who picked the songs. What
did he want?

"Hurry! I want my friend see you sing
something good."

"Actually, I found that last song very

nice," Jack commented.

"No, you did not!" Gleefak slammed his fist on the table, causing it to tremble beneath them both and rattle the poor cage. Rachel nearly toppled over. "You can't like that song. No! She is my singer. Mine! You do not like her silly, dumb songs. Only the songs I like do you like."

Jack's eyebrows shot to his forehead, and Rachel noticed the jagged red scar on the side of it. What had he done?

"Well, then, perhaps we should let her choose something more uplifting and fun. Something you would like." She heard the chuckle in Jack's voice. She could tell he thought the giant was acting like a little child.

Jack glanced at her and they shared a smile.

Gleeflak slammed his hand down on the table again, and this time the action startled the baby so much that she began to cry. "Enough! I do not like this game! We are done. Rachel, you go back to your cage now!"

"Are you sure?" She had never seen him this angry before.

"Yes! And you go in there with her!" He

stood Jack up and pushed him toward her. "You need locked up too! You both bad. And you are not my friend!"

Jack turned and asked, "Me? Why?"

The giant pointed to him. "Because you like her! And you not allowed to like my singer. Only I like her!"

"I am sorry," Jack said. "She is very pretty. And she sings wonderfully. It is hard not to like her."

"Get in there!"

Gleeflak's face turned so red, Rachel ran over to the cage as quickly as possible. The poor baby was really crying now. Rachel fumbled with the lock, but could not grasp such a large thing on her own.

Jack stepped up behind her and together they pushed the release until it clicked and opened. "Does he act like this often?" he asked.

"No. I have never seen him lose his temper the whole time I have been here." She stepped into the cage and waited for him to enter as well.

"How has Verity been holding up?"

"Who?"

"The baby. Her name is Verity."

The little girl ran to Rachel and wrapped her arms around her legs. She stopped crying immediately. "How do you know that?" she asked.

"The witch who helped me get to you claims the baby is hers and wants her back."

"Oh, dear. You bargained with a witch?"

"I had no choice." He knelt down and held out his arms. "Can I hold her? Will she come to me?"

"You could try." Rachel gently pushed against the baby's shoulder. "Do you want to see Jack?"

"Verity," he called. "Come here."

She clung to Rachel's dress, but peeked over at him when she heard her name.

"Call her again."

"Verity, come here. I will not hurt you. May I hold you, please?"

She turned around more fully and giggled before tucking her head back into Rachel's dress. "Is that your name?" Rachel grinned down at the little darling below her. "Did Jack say your name?"

Verity giggled again and nodded.

"Would you like to go see him?"

Verity turned around and this time got a bit braver and let go of the dress to walk up to Jack.

"Come on," he said. "Let me give you a hug."

Slowly, while glancing back at Rachel for support, she walked into Jack's arms. Her little frame being folded into his chest as he stood up with her nearly caused Rachel's heart to burst. "You are a sweetheart," she whispered.

"She certainly is." He rubbed his chin upon her bouncy curls.

Rachel chuckled softly, a warm glow spreading all through her. "I meant you, Jack. You are a sweetheart to care about such a little one. It makes me happy to see you this way."

"Enough!" Gleeflak cried into the cage from where he had been watching them.

Verity snuggled in closer to Jack, who whispered to her.

Rachel watched as the giant locked them in and then lifted the whole thing up. It tilted wildly to the right.

"Sit down!" Jack called out as he did so

himself. "And hold on to the golden bars. I believe this is not going to be a pleasant ride."

CHAPTER FIFTEEN

ONCE GLEEFLAK HAD GONE, carrying Jack and Rachel and the baby in the cage, Jill came in from outside and snuck into the great living area, hiding herself within a tall bookshelf. She assumed the giant would be back with them all eventually, and she did not want to be too far away—or on the other side of a closed door—when it was time to rescue them. Having overheard most of the conversation from behind the pillar in the courtyard, she was amazed at Jack's quick thinking and his interactions with the large man.

Gleeflak even believed they were friends!

She grinned as she climbed up and sat atop a grouping of books that were nearly as tall as she was within the shadows of the shelf. Pulling off her pack, she rummaged for some food and began to eat dried meat and a bit of an apple. Her eyes roamed around the elegant room as she marveled at its sumptuous décor. Honestly, the giant was quite a simpleton— how could anyone of such a small mind even think of such luxuries? It did not make sense that he would be so picky or refined in his tastes.

Huh. She wondered a bit more, trying to piece together the oddity of it all, when commotion from a room down the hall made her pause. Gleeflak was shouting at someone. He was angry. Goodness. She glanced around the room, realizing he might be coming back any moment now. Was there something, anything she could use to defend herself or Jack and Rachel if need be?

Upon a carved end table across the room sat a letter opener which would serve as a very nice sword, if somewhat heavy, but she was too far away from it now. On her left was a long, tasseled curtain tieback that looked like a thick rope. That might do!

The shouting grew louder as she jumped from the bookshelf and ran to the dangling lanyard. Climbing up the rope, she quickly unhooked it from its gold catch attached to the wall and allowed it to fall to the ground as she slid down the length of the blue velvet curtain.

She heard steps right outside the door. Gleeflak was here!

Jill did not have to time to collect the tieback or hide it. Instead, she left it right upon the floor and climbed up the shelf, tucking herself into the spot above the books. She made sure the pack was hidden within the shadows as well and peered out toward the door just as the giant walked in, swinging the large cage.

She heard shouting and looked in the golden cage to find Rachel and Jack holding on to the bars while it swung wildly back and forth, the furniture in the cage careening into them. As the giant came closer to her shelf, she held her breath and scrunched in tighter. The cage drew closer into view and just before it was lifted to perch somewhere above her, she saw that Jack was holding the witch's baby with one arm and the bar with the other.

Jill heard a great slamming noise as Gleeflak shouted, "There! This is where bad people stay. You stay here and think about how bad you are all night."

She watched his legs as they stepped back before the sound of Rachel's voice caused him to pause. "Do we get supper?" she asked.

The giant knees began to quake before he announced, "No! No supper for anyone! And not for you either, Jack! You are bad!"

"I am sorry you feel that way," he answered above her.

"No, you aren't. But you will be sorry. Tomorrow I'll drop you off the edge of this land and you can go back to your village." He laughed. "You'll be dead and smushed! It will teach you to come here to my castle and like my singing girl! She is mine! Mine! No one likes her but me!"

Silence followed as the giant remained there. Jill had no idea what was happening, but wished he would leave so she could help Jack and Rachel. Gleeflak stayed there for some time. It was more than likely just a few minutes, but being scrunched up and desperate not to breathe too loudly, it seemed to Jill to be an age at least. What was he doing?

Just when she thought he would never leave, the giant turned to her left and walked toward the long curtain tieback upon the ground.

No!

But he must not have seen the rope because in the next instant, he was walking through it—which was much worse! His front foot got caught in the loops of the cord while the back foot stepped directly on the thing, tightening the rope around his front ankle as he lifted it, making the large man shift and teeter and lose his balance. He crashed with a loud thump, sprawled across the ground.

"WHHHAAAATTTTT?" roared the giant as Jill cringed and covered her ears.

The baby began to cry.

"Who did this? Who left this on the ground so I would fall and get hurt?"

Sitting up, Gleeflak rubbed his knees and removed the offending cords. When he was free, he grunted and groaned and stood back up. His loud, clomping footsteps brought him up to the bookshelf again. "Who did that? Who?"

When they did not answer, Jill saw his hand rise and then lower, carrying the cage. Inside she could see Jack frantically placing the baby within what looked to be a big music box. He stuffed blankets and the like in with her, and then clicked the lid in place. The last thing she saw was him reaching for Rachel before the giant carried them out of her vision as he turned away, giving her a view of his rather large backside.

"You are not my friends!" he suddenly shouted before swinging the cage around in a wide circle.

No! Jill wanted to scream. *No!*

The giant let go and the cage flew across the room, slamming into a wall and then tumbling down to the floor behind a large settee.

"Oh, my word! Jack! Rachel!" she whispered behind her hands, covering her mouth. Shock and horror raced through her whole body. What had he done? What had he done?

Then the door slammed shut behind Gleeflak as he walked out.

CHAPTER SIXTEEN

AS RAPIDLY AS POSSIBLE, Jill made her way off the shelf and over to the fallen cage. It was bent and damaged significantly on the outside. "Hello?" she whispered as she crept closer to the dented bottom. She could hear the faint sound of the baby crying. "Jack? Rachel?"

She walked around the underside of the cage, her heart beating frantically at the sight of the insides in such disarray. There looked to be a bed of some sort tossed on its side with blankets and pillows everywhere. The music box was upside down and the cries of the baby sounded muffled.

Jill swiftly made her way to the broken door of the cage and climbed inside. She could tell the baby was frantic. Hurrying over to the pretty box, she tugged against it, trying to flip it over. At least the baby was still alive.

"Urgh," she grunted. It was too heavy. She needed her brother's help.

"Jack?" she called. Glancing around the ruined place, she began tossing pillows and blankets aside. "Jack? Rachel?"

She heard a soft moan behind her and whipped around to see who it was. "Rachel?" she asked as she approached the doubled-over form, Rachel's long pale hair streaming down her back. There was a mattress over her head and arms that Jill quickly pulled off to reveal a beaten-up Jack, his hands still clasping Rachel's. "Jack!" she called, but he did not move an inch. He was lying on his side, flush against the bars of the cage. It looked as though he had tried to absorb as much of the impact as he could to protect Rachel.

Rachel groaned again. She slowly pulled her hands out of his and pushed her way to a sitting position. Rubbing her face, she brushed aside the hair that was covering it, exposing a large welt running down her forehead, cheek, and neck.

The baby's howls were becoming desperate.

She looked at her brother. *Please do not let him be dead. Please do not let him be dead!* "Jack!" Jill cried as she rushed forward and pressed her hands against his chest. "Jack! Wake up!" It was then that she noticed one of his legs was bent awkwardly.

"What is that sound?" Rachel muttered. "And Jill! How long have you been here?"

Jill decided now was not the time to answer useless questions. "The sound is the baby. She needs help. Right now."

"Verity?" Rachel sat up more fully. "Where is she?"

Jill pointed. "In the box, but I cannot lift it. Jack! Jack!"

"Goodness!" Rachel looked around and, seeing the music box, pulled herself all the way up, clinging to the bars. "Help me," she called.

Jill left her brother and hurried over. Together they heaved and pushed with all their might until they were able to lift the box on its side, with the latch at the top.

The baby screamed in fright at the movement, her muffled cries growing in intensity.

"Hush, Verity," Rachel cooed as she unlocked the thing. "I am coming. It is almost over, baby."

The lid sprang open and a very red-faced, sweaty Verity, along with several pillows, came toppling out. Jill leaped forward and caught the baby up in her arms. For such a little thing, she could surely cry. After a few moments of the girl's tears, Rachel held out her arms and Jill gratefully passed the child on before hastening back to her brother.

"Jack!" she called. "Jack!" This time she yanked on his broad shoulders to try to wake him.

"No." Rachel fell to her knees, the baby cradled against her. She gasped. "No. Do not tell me he is gone. He cannot die while I yet live. He cannot. He saved me—he saved me and the baby."

Jill took a deep breath. "We do not know if he is dead. There is not time for theatrics until we know he is truly gone." She hovered her hand over his mouth and nose to see if any air was coming out. She could feel nothing. Looking around the area, she found a thin piece of gold about the size of her palm that had come off the door. Placing that just above his mouth and nose, she watched while Rachel sniffled, calming her tears.

Please let him live.

Please let him live.

Please let him live.

Just as she was about to give up, a small cloud of steam from his breath formed itself upon the gold. Yes. He was alive. "He is just stunned!" She smiled at Rachel. "He is alive."

"Thank the heavens!" Rachel collapsed against the mattress that was tossed aside and leaning upright against the cage. "What do we do now?"

"I do not know, but I imagine whatever we decide, we better make it quick before the giant comes back."

Rachel grimaced. "Who knows what he will do to us then!" She looked down at the child in her arms. Verity had stopped crying and was down to a few fast-paced whimpers now that she was safe again.

"The poor baby," Jill whispered. "What a rough time of it she has had."

Rachel shook her head. "You have no idea. I cannot imagine what would have become of her if I had not been captured too. It breaks my heart just thinking of the fear she has experienced already."

"Well, there is no need for any more suffering. We have to get out of here." Jill glanced over at Jack, seeing again that his leg was twisted. She leaned over and positioned it better. "It would be wise for us to think of a way to get him out of this castle on our own, in case he does not wake up."

"He has to wake up. We cannot do it without him. He has to."

Jill saw the golden cage door and walked over to it. "What if we dragged him on something like this?" Tugging on it, she saw that it weighed too much to pull on her own. "Never mind. I had forgotten how heavy gold is until this moment." She walked around the settee to see what else could be of use in the room. When her eyes alighted on the curtain tieback still lying upon the floor, she quickly snatched it up and dragged the whole thing behind the sofa. "What about this? I was hoping to hide it earlier, but he came back too soon."

"So it was you who caused Gleeflak to fall!" Rachel gasped. "We had no clue what he was even speaking about."

"I did not plan it. I merely wanted to use the rope to escape, but did not have enough time to conceal it with me." Jill lugged it up to Jack. "Here, help me entwine these together in a series of knots to make a suitable mesh to drag him."

"You mean to leave sometime tonight, before Gleeflak wakes up in the morning?"

"No." Jill shook her head. "I mean to leave this instant. We do not know if he will come back again to check on you once he realizes what he has done. Hopefully we will be long gone if he does."

CHAPTER SEVENTEEN

THE GIRLS SCURRIED TO intertwine the long tieback into netting. It took just over a quarter of an hour to accomplish the chore, and then the tricky part was figuring how best to get Jack on it. After another good ten minutes, Jack was on the mesh with little Verity giggling upon his chest. Jill's pack was used to block off the lower end so the child would not tumble out without them aware.

Rachel pulled one corner while Jill took the other. Once they were able to get the net moving, it was quite simple to keep up a fast-paced movement due to the silky ropes, and ended up being an easier challenge than either expected. They were through the crack in the door and out of the palace courtyard, sliding through the castle gates, before even a full five minutes had passed.

"This is perfect!" Jill exclaimed as they went on the path leading to the beanstalk.

Jack groaned.

What was happening to him?

It felt as though he were traveling *under* a carriage instead of *in* it.

Oomph! He winced as his back hit another stone and risked opening his eyes. The late-afternoon sunshine was blocked by slowly passing treetops. Indeed, he was traveling, but not as fast as it felt like, and certainly not as fast as a carriage.

He heard giggles and glanced down. There perched happily on his chest was sweet little Verity in all her brown curls. "Well, hello there," he croaked in barely a whisper.

Making out the chattering of Jill and Rachel above him, he looked up to see what was going on. They both seemed to be pulling on a blue net of some kind and merrily babbling away.

"Hello?" he croaked again, but they did not hear him.

Just then they went over another rock, and this time it jabbed him directly in his shoulder. "Ahhh!" he cried out. Something must be wrong with his arm. That should not have hurt so badly.

"Jack!"

The moving stopped, and Rachel was hovering over him when he opened his eyes. "You are awake! Finally!"

He grinned and brought a hand up to run his fingers through the long blonde hair spilling upon him. "Yes." Tugging softly on a section of her locks, he brought her head forward, eager to taste her lips after so long.

"Jack!" She laughed and mockingly scolded him. "We cannot kiss now—the baby will be flattened."

"Jill, help a man out," he called, his eyes never leaving Rachel's. "I have not been able to kiss my fiancée properly this whole day."

His sister chuckled as she removed Verity from his chest, and Jack wasted no time in bringing his beautiful Rachel to his lips.

"I love you," he murmured against her mouth. "I love you more each time I see you."

"Hmm…" She sighed and kissed him back before raising her head and saying, "I love you as well. Though, if you scare me like that again and pretend to be dead when you are merely asleep, I shall kill you."

"What?" He smirked. "Come here, you." He pulled her down and kissed that delicious mouth once more.

"This is good, but perhaps heading home would be better," Jill interrupted.

Rachel smiled and pulled back. "She does have a point."

Jack struggled to sit up. "How long have I been unconscious?"

"About an hour or so, I imagine," Jill answered. "How are you feeling? Your leg was pretty crooked; do you think you could walk?"

"My leg?" He moved them both with ease. "What are you talking about?"

"Truly? Perhaps the angle you were lying in made it seem worse than it was." Jill held out her hand. "Here, allow us to assist you and we will see if you can stand."

Rachel held her arm out as well and he grasped both hands as they hauled him to a standing position. He winced as fire ripped through his shoulder, but did not cry out again—no reason to alarm the girls. But he knew his left shoulder was painfully wrenched.

Stepping forward, he was happy to note his legs were fine. One ankle was definitely tender, which caused him to hop a bit, but nothing he could not shake off. He would put his full weight on in it a few minutes' time. He held out his arms and turned for the girls' inspection. "I am well. Do you see? Now let us get going before Gleeflak decides he would like to be friends again."

He bent over and collected the mesh. Did they really do this by themselves? "Have I ever told you both how decidedly ingenious you are?" he asked as he looked up.

"Do not stare at me!" Rachel exclaimed. "It was all Jill's doing. If it were up to me, we would still be in that crooked cage waiting for the giant to come back."

Jill brushed the comment aside. "No,

Rachel is being silly."

"I am not. I had decided I would find a way out of the palace on my own if I had to, but when the time came to escape, it was the furthest thing from my mind. I tell you, Jill is incredibly resourceful."

His sister blushed. "And have you met Jack?" she asked. "He taught me everything I know."

"Yes, well, we could sit and compliment each other all day—and I see you females would prefer to do just that—but let us get this baby wrapped up and go home!"

Jill laughed while turning to Rachel. "And then there are days when I cannot stand the man and I want to kill him. But I usually do not mention such things in the company of my friends."

Chuckling, Rachel shook her head. "Believe me, I know all about wanting to throttle him. The thought passes my mind quite often."

"And you both love me dearly for it. I know." He collected the rest of the netting, and while tossing it aside said, "If one of you will strap Verity to my back using Jill's pack, we can be on our way."

"How right you are! He is just like you!" Rachel said as she helped reposition the food items and settled the baby inside.

They readjusted the wrapping of the pack to allow Verity's legs to dangle out, and then placed it on him.

Jack bit back the pain as his arm twisted when he put the pack on, but thank goodness Verity did not weigh much and so did not overly burden that shoulder. "Are all of my womenfolk ready, then? Can we finally leave now?" He grinned at them.

Jill rolled her eyes and pushed past him. "We have been ready for ages. We have been waiting upon you, sleepyhead."

Rachel laughed as she approached him, sliding her hand into his. "Yes. Take me home."

"Very well." He bounced the baby a bit to adjust her better and then they were off.

In no time at all, they were approaching the tips of the tall beanstalk.

"So this is how you arrived here?" Rachel exclaimed.

"Well, when one bargains with a witch,

one should never be surprised at what means one is given to complete the task," Jack replied as he looped one leg around the stalk and began to climb down. "It is quite safe," he called back. "Jill, help Rachel tie her skirts up so she will not get caught on the leaves and such."

It was much easier to climb down than it had been to go up, and as long as Jack stayed at the bottom of the group, he figured he could catch one if she should fall. The sun was close to setting as they neared the base of the beanstalk and first heard the great roar of Gleeflak.

"Jack?" Jill had never sounded more frightened.

"Yes, I heard. Let us move—quickly now."

CHAPTER EIGHTEEN

THE GROUP MOVED DOWN the stalk at a much more rapid pace than before. All at once, nothing mattered but the safety of the village spread out below them.

"We are almost there!" Jill shouted.

"Hurry!" Jack answered back. "Do not dawdle—move faster!"

He was about two hundred feet from the ground when he noticed a roaring coming from below. He glanced down and saw a large group assembled, hopefully to welcome them home. It would seem that word had spread far and wide—they were clapping and cheering.

Jack felt the trembling of the stalk the instant Gleeflak climbed on it. "Go, girls! Now. We have no more time. He is on the stalk with us!"

"We felt him!" Rachel called out as she jumped from coiled stalk to coiled stalk.

"Help!" Jack shouted to the group. They were cheering so loudly, no one heard. "Stop!" he attempted again. "Please stop! We need help!" He was nearing close to about fifty feet from the ground, the girls much higher up, when someone finally heard him and hushed the group.

"What?" the man shouted after the crowd calmed down.

"Get as many men together as you can," Jack called, still climbing downward. "And fetch axes. The giant is on this stalk with us. We must hurry and chop it down!"

The men ran, and as Jack stepped off the stalk, the girls some forty or sixty feet above, some of the men had already returned with their axes. "Begin now. But start in the back," he called out. "The girls will be fine on this side. Hurry!"

"Jack!" his mother called as she ran up

to him. "You did it! You saved them!" He hugged her and then she gasped, pulling back. "My goodness! And a baby, too. What in the world?"

Oh. He had almost forgotten about Verity. "Here. I will explain later," he said as he shucked off the pack and removed the sleeping baby. "Take her and see that she is fed and changed. She is no doubt soiled, for we have not stopped once." He handed her over and turned to leave before remembering. "Oh, and Mother, her name is Verity."

He watched his mother grin at the baby a moment before glancing at his father, who had just come up the hill. "Do you mind helping Rachel and Jill down while I chop? Someone will need to be here."

"Yes, I can do it." Hansel touched his son's shoulder. "Well done, you. I am a proud father right now."

Jack met his father's eyes and nodded. "As soon as the girls are down and you can fetch an axe, we could use you too."

Hansel lifted up his axe from the ground and handed one to his son. "I am already with you, my boy."

They shared a smile and Jack ran around to the back of the stalk. He began hacking into his own section immediately. The cheer that came from the crowd let him know the girls had made it safely upon the ground, and with that, he really put his back into it and whacked with all his might.

The pain in his wrenched shoulder was unbearable. However, nothing compared to the vengeance of a spoiled giant who wanted revenge. Jack's limbs would heal; losing those he loved most would not.

As he chopped, he unexpectedly noticed a strange, magical mist swirling around his head. He pulled back. *What is that?*

Suddenly the witch appeared before him in a puff of white smoke. "Where is Verity?" she demanded. "Where is she?"

"Are you truly this selfish? I am trying to save us all. Gleeflak is on his way down. Move!" Jack shouted.

She yanked on his axe. "I want her! Tell me you saved her! You promised you would."

"Yes. She is safe."

"Where?" She looked around. "Where is she? I need her right this moment!"

"No. You will have to wait." He pointed out toward the field behind him. "Now, leave me!"

Cora looked at his shoulder, and he could feel a slight tingly sensation where it was wrenched. He watched as she smiled, and then felt a fiery pain surge through his whole arm and settle into the torn tissues.

"Ahhh!" he groaned. It felt as though she were ripping his arm clean from his body. Beads of sweat popped onto his brow as he bowed under the pressure.

Just then a great roar could be heard above and the pain released.

"Gleeflak!" She glanced up, and then spoke urgently, "Meet me next to your home with that baby as soon as this beanstalk is felled, or more than your arm will come off!" With that, she disappeared as quickly as she had come.

Jack gritted his teeth and lunged and smacked and walloped over and over again until he finally gave a massive shout. The new damage to his arm and the weight of the axe were too much. Falling to his knees, he simply could not do it. Another moment and he might become unconscious again.

Hansel rushed to his side. "Son! What is wrong?"

"My shoulder. It is wrenched and I am too weak to continue."

"What is that?" asked his father, pointing toward Jack's shirt. "Is that what I think it is?"

Jack looked down and saw the vial dangling from its leather cord. It must have slipped out. "The potion Cora gave Grandfather," he said. "Why?"

Hansel looked up at the large stalk, then over at the men who were only a quarter of the way through it. "You are a genius!" he suddenly exclaimed. "Quick, hand it to me!"

Jack slipped it off with his good arm. "Here. What do you mean to do with it?"

"Watch," his father replied as he popped the cork off the top. "I hope this still works." He then shook and splattered all of the contents onto the beanstalk. Walking around the men, he made sure as many of the vines were touched by the droplets as possible.

"Is something supposed to happen?" Jack asked when his father returned.

"Your mother did something similar with

some enchanted grass that had grown and held me captive. The potion caused the grass to shrivel up immediately."

Suddenly the men began to bellow.

Jack looked up. The stalk teetered and swayed. "Run!" he shouted as he scrambled to his feet.

His father pulled him out of the way just before the whole beanstalk crashed to the ground in a long, crooked line, barely skimming past houses and upsetting farms.

THE MEN OF THE village searched through the ruined beanstalk for hours, but never found the remains of the giant. However, they did find the dead body of the witch an hour or so after the beanstalk fell. She was the only person crushed to death by the stalk.

"Jack, do you know this woman?" one of his father's friends asked as he laid Cora's body upon the ground. Jack, hoping to help clean up the mess, had just come from the cottage where his shoulder had been wrapped by the village doctor. Twilight was fading quickly and soon it would be completely dark.

"Yes. Where was she?"

"Near your home, under the fattest portion of the stalk. That is why we thought you might know her, since she was strangely nearby and yet not with the crowd of people who were standing out of harm's way."

"Thank you for bringing her to me. We will take care of her burial."

When the men walked away, Jack called his father and together they marveled at the woman who had never died—until now, of course.

"Do not tell your grandfather. There is no reason for him to believe that she was not already dead."

Jack nodded. "I wondered if it would make him more anxious, imagining what Cora might have been up to all these years."

"Precisely. Though, do not discount this woman. She has clearly come back from Hades once—who knows what mischief she has left behind for us. Or why she found the need to visit us again."

"Pa, she returned for Verity."

"Verity? The little angel. She was Cora's?"

"I believe Cora stole her from someone else, but I did not ask her about it—I did not wish to risk her wrath. And even though I have never seen it happen, it is said the baby has the gift of turning things to gold."

Hansel whistled. "The Midas touch?"

"Yes, exactly. But I am almost certain it is just a rumor floating about."

"Is that why the giant wanted her?"

"Yes."

"And Cora?"

"Aye. Can you think of the greed that would be shown by the rest of the world if Verity could do what it has been claimed she can? They would all want her for themselves."

His father's gaze grew serious. "No one can ever know who this child is."

Jack smiled. "And since you are so very good at hiding vulnerable children—or so I have heard—do you think you and Mother would consider taking her in, now that Cora is gone?"

"I think we had better ask your mother first."

"Will you tell Mother of the danger Verity may be in?"

"She would have my hide if I kept such a secret from her!"

Jack grinned and then glanced up when Rachel walked over.

Hansel patted Jack on his wrapped shoulder. "Go and be with your dearest. I have some baby news to impart to your mother."

CHAPTER NINETEEN

JACK WALKED AWAY, LEAVING the dead witch upon the ground, and pulled Rachel with him. They went down the lane and over to their favorite tree just as the stars were beginning to come into full glory.

"You know, I wished upon those stars while I was in that castle," she whispered. "I would wish upon them every night."

"And what did you hope for?" he asked as he wrapped his good arm around her and snuggled her to his heart.

"I yearned, more than anything, to see you again."

He leaned down and kissed her light hair. "I love you. I would never have left you there."

She clutched his shirt and nodded. "I know."

"Rachel?"

"Hmm?"

"Are you sure you would still like to marry me?"

"What?" She pulled back and looked at him.

He thought of how the witch plotted out this entire escapade. "I cannot guarantee our life will be normal. In fact, I am certain we will face many adventures, even things that are so very terrifying. Rachel, I am afraid I cannot protect you and shield you from all the scary things that may happen."

She leaned up and kissed his mouth before stating simply, "Life is about the adventure, darling. And I will gladly face anything as long as I am with you. We cannot run from bad experiences or keep things from happening to us. Dreadful things must happen to everyone. But it is the people who care for us the most who guarantee we will not be left alone when dark trials come. I love you, Jack, and I count down the thirty-two days remaining until I am Mrs. Waithwrite. Do you know why? Because I know you will never allow me to suffer alone."

It was sometime later before the two sweethearts were through being sweet and had calmed their hearts from the kisses they rained upon the other.

WHEN JACK RETURNED FROM walking Rachel home, he made his way over to the fallen stalk to look for the body of Cora. It took several turns and retraced steps before he realized the worst.

"Father!" he called out as he ran to the darkened cottage. "Pa, are you awake?"

"Yes?" came the sleepy reply as Jack burst into the home.

He quickly made his way to his parents' room. "Did you bury Cora?" he asked.

"Cora?"

"Yes! The witch. Did you bury her?"

"No. I did not. I was too exhausted. I figured you and I would do so in the morning.

Why?"

Jack took a deep breath. "She is gone."

GLEEFLAK WAS NEVER HEARD from again. Many say he must have felt the tremors of the multiple axes chopping down the stalk and quickly climbed back up. Others believe he disappeared in a puff of smoke, like the witch. And still others believe it was all a hoax brought on by Rachel and Jack's families to guarantee they had a larger-than-normal wedding party and therefore, more gifts.

The young couple did have an excessively large marriage celebration, due to the many onlookers and gawkers who came to see the brave couple in person. And though their life was full of trials, some of them much harder than they expected, they happily chose to walk together and support and uplift each other through it all.

They eventually went on to have three strapping boys of their own, all determined to find their personal adventures—especially when they heard the tales of their parents and grandparents. It was to be expected, they were sure, that they would have their very own fine tales to tell one day.

Jill settled down quite nicely with an excellent lord from the court. Due to all the praise and popularity her family found, she had a slew of eligible men to choose from. But after sorting through them for a few years, she finally settled on the best one of all. He was kind, yet strong enough to handle the feisty, headstrong girl—and most importantly, he loved every moment of it. They went on to have five beautiful children who enjoyed playing with their cousins and following them about on their adventures.

Little Verity grew to be a beautiful young lady who did have a very peculiar gift that many found to be excessively pleasing and desired her for themselves. She was saved, however, by true love—but her adventure will be shared another day, when the time for such a story as hers can be told properly. It will most definitely be its own book, *The Princess with the Golden Touch*.

But as for now, this is the ending of the tale of Jack, the bravest man in the land, who, with the help of his fearless sister, bargained with a witch and outwitted a giant to save the only woman he had ever loved. And they, my dear readers, I know for an absolute fact, lived happily ever after.

THE END

Snow White

Chapter One

RAVEN LAUGHED AS SHE looked back at her new sister, Snow. They were the best of friends and had been for years—now she could not believe her luck! Sisters, truly sisters—it seemed like a magical wish come true. They had imagined and dreamed of it, and it was finally a reality. Snow's father had proposed less than four months ago to Raven's mother, Queen Melantha Flynn, a beautiful, widowed woman with two children.

Not that they were still children. Corlan was nearly twenty-two and Raven and Snow were both in their late teens, but Snow's father would always consider them children. Raven watched as her beautiful new sister ran up to her, her long black curls bobbing as she came. There was not one person in Snow's kingdom who had not instantly become enamored with the girl. She had a special quality about her—a naivety and zest for life, an inner joy—something that radiated from her happy smile and wound itself about the hearts of all those who were near her.

"It has finally happened!" Snow exclaimed as she wrapped her arms around Raven and hugged her tightly.

"I know, I know! I cannot believe today has come at last!"

Snow pulled back, her full red lips arching in a pretty smile against her pale skin, her black lashes fluttering briefly over her brilliant blue eyes. She was a stunning beauty. If Raven did not love her as much as she did, she would find the green tinges of jealously invading her thoughts, but as it was, she simply could not think ill of the enchanting Snow White. No one could.

"Where is Corlan?" Snow grinned. "I

must hug my new brother as well."

Raven glanced over to where Corlan stood, watching them intently, his eyes never straying from Snow. He had been head over heels for the girl since they were children. Long before their parents had agreed to marry, King Herbert, Snow's father, had often brought her to play with them, the neighboring royal children, so she could experience friendship. He worried that without her mother, she would become too sad and lose the finer elegant qualities needed to turn into a lady and ruler one day. And so he hoped to bring her out of the melancholy of losing her dear mother and into the warmth of the Flynn court.

"He is over there." Raven nodded toward her brother.

She grinned at Corlan's reaction as the stunning girl rushed toward him and threw her arms about his shoulders. He held her and closed his eyes briefly, no doubt reveling in the feel of her so close to him.

Snow pulled back, and Raven loved the way her brother's eyes observed that lively face before him, watching each movement, each smile, each word as it came from her lips.

When would he tell her he was in love? Raven had been asking him for months now, but he would never answer. Just then, a dashing young man stepped forward and bowed low before the pretty princess in her red-and-gold gown.

"Princess Snow," Raven heard him say, "will you do me the honor of dancing the first set with me?"

Raven glanced around the grand ballroom. It would seem indeed that it was time to begin the entertainment her mother had requested. Several couples already lined the outskirts of the floor, waiting for the king and new queen to begin their nuptial dance.

"Snow is dancing with me for the first set," Corlan answered.

Raven looked over at her brother. Bravo. He stood just a bit taller, with his arm wrapped around Snow's shoulders.

Snow smiled sweetly at the man. "I promise to go out on the floor with you during the second."

The man glanced from Snow to Corlan and then back to Snow again. He must have liked the smile on her face, for he bowed lower and said, "Your Highness, there is nothing I wish for more."

She nodded, and then looked up at Corlan.

"Shall we?" he asked.

They really did make an incredible couple. Corlan was so tall and dashing, with his distinguished brown hair and lightly sun-kissed skin and deep green eyes. He was a sight to behold. But Snow, bless her heart, did not ever appear to prefer one man over the other. She seemed completely oblivious to the male species altogether—enjoying them, of course, and smiling serenely and capturing their hearts one by one. But every suitor who came to stare and try his hand for the fair princess left with a confused look on his face, for they simply did not know what to make of her. Did she not like them? Did they do something wrong? She seemed happy enough, but pushed away their advances as if they were nothing to her. Again and again, Raven watched princes from all over the continent come and try their best to woo her, but to no avail.

"King Herbert and Queen Melantha will now take the floor," the herald announced grandly.

Raven watched her mother, a stunning red-haired beauty glorious in pale-gold silk, step into the arms of her beloved Herbert as they began to waltz on the floor of the sparkling chandeliered room. The guests exclaimed over the couple as they passed by, tittering behind fans and whispering of their happiness for the great king and queen.

They had sent a surge of new hope throughout the land by uniting the two kingdoms. Raven could feel the excitement and joy buzzing through the air in pings of awareness at the exhilaration this wedding brought to all.

Raven smiled as her mother came near and then dipped and spun away as the music wound down. Even though she was in her early forties, there was no woman who could claim to have the beauty she still possessed—a vision of loveliness from her shining head of hair to her dainty, nimble feet.

The first set of dances were about to begin. Raven sighed and looked around the room, her heart clenching slightly within her chest. So many of the couples were already eagerly waiting to take their places on the dance floor. She had hoped that by now, a young man would have been inclined to ask for her hand during this particular set, today of all days when it was her mother's wedding. But no young man made his way toward her. Indeed, most of them were across the room, keenly watching Snow and Corlan speak softly and laugh with one another.

It was no use. There would never be a man who saw her while her dear new sister was in the room. Taking a deep breath, she blinked back a few tears and attempted to paste on a smile. She refused to become a silly water pot today, when truly everything she could have wished for came true. This was the happiest day of her life.

"Excuse me, Princess Raven Flynn?" a dashing young man asked as he walked toward her and then bowed.

Butterflies flurried wildly within her chest. "Yes?" she replied a little breathlessly. He was unbelievably handsome, with his blond hair and deep brown eyes.

"Forgive me for being so forward and not waiting for a proper introduction. I am Prince

Terrance from the Sybright court and was pointed in your direction. I was wondering if you knew if the Princess Snow White was free this set? I have only just arrived, by invitation of King Herbert, and have been eager to meet this paragon I have heard mentioned."

"Oh." Her smile tightened. "Of course." She nodded, reminding herself that someone as attractive as he would only ever wish to be with Snow. "She is engaged at present," she said as the dancers began to walk upon the floor. "But if you wait your turn, she is indeed very amiable and would be more than happy to stand up with you."

"Perfect." He smiled, showing off two adorable dimples as he did so.

Raven gasped, and then quickly bit her lip to keep from doing it again. She had always longed for a man with dimples.

Terrance grinned down at her, those indentations only deepening more. "Are you perchance free at the moment?" he asked, looking around as if amazed she was still standing with him and not upon the floor.

"Yes, I am."

"And do you mean to dance?"

"Of course I do."

He took a pace back and swept another bow. "Forgive me, princess! I did not realize. Please, would you do me the honor of stepping out with me?"

She giggled. "I would be delighted," she said as she placed her hand within his and walked onto the floor.

ABOUT THE AUTHOR

JENNI JAMES IS THE busy mom of seven rambunctious children ranging from the ages of 2 to 16. When she isn't chasing them around her house in sunny New Mexico, she is dreaming of new books to write. She loves to hear from her readers and can be contacted at:

jenni@authorjennijames.com, or by writing to:

Jenni James
PO Box 514
Farmington, NM 87499

Follow Jenni James on:
www.facebook.com/authorjennijames to find out when new releases are coming!

13274685R00095

Printed in Great Britai
by Amazon.co.uk, Ltd
Marston Gate.